Shane Brown was born in 1974 and lives in Norwich, UK. He received a doctorate in Film, Television and Media from the University of East Anglia in 2014. He is the author of *Breaking Point* a young adult novel about homophobic bullying, as well as *Elvis Presley: A Listener's Guide* and *Bobby Darin: A Listener's Guide.*

Follow the author on Twitter @shanebrown74.

Cover photo: Roberto David

BREAKING DOWN
A sequel to *Breaking Point*

Shane Brown

CHAPTER ONE

James Marsh took a deep breath and then mentioned something he had wanted to talk about for the previous forty-five minutes.

"I saw Jason today," he said

"What happened?"

"I went into the newsagent's, just to pick up some milk for Mum. He had his back to me, so I didn't see him at first. It was a bit awkward when he turned around and we saw each other. He smiled at me, paid for his stuff, and left. I've seen him around before, in Tesco and that, but it's easy enough to avoid each other in somewhere like that. You just go down another aisle and pretend you didn't see him. You can't do that in a tiny newsagent's. You have to acknowledge each other."

James took a sip of water, and waited for his counsellor to respond.

"What do you think when you see him? Does it bother you?" she said.

"I still hate him, if that's what you mean. I don't think I will ever do anything else. I'm not about to shake hands and be best friends. But…"

James stared out across the room, his concentration lapsing for a moment. It wasn't an unusual occurrence.

"But what?"

James looked back at the counsellor.

"But he looks sad. And lonely. And I guess he probably is. And I know what that can feel like. And I don't wish that, even on him. I don't know who his friends are, these days. If he has any. None of the crowd he went around with at school. There was only Smithy left anyway, and I know Jason hasn't had anything to do with him since the night on the bridge. As far as I know, he just broke off all contact with him. With everyone, I think. It's weird. But perhaps that's what he felt he had to do to move on."

The truth was that James didn't know *what* he felt about Jason Mitchell any more, the boy who had made his life hell more than two years earlier. It seemed so long ago now, and yet those events still tended to dominate his life without him fully admitting it. The nightmares, the panic attacks, the distrust of other people. James was sure that Jason was to blame for all of that. And he was definitely to blame for James going to counselling sessions week after week. But, in his efforts to try and forget him, he talked about him for an hour a week. Sometimes it seemed like a backward logic.

"Do you feel sorry for him?" the counsellor asked.

"Sometimes." James smiled. "He screwed his life up. You only get one shot at it. That sounds stupid, right?"

The counsellor shrugged her shoulders.

"You feel what you feel. You've told me that you were lonely at school. It's only natural to feel empathy for someone else in the same position, isn't it?"

"I don't know. Not considering he ruined my life for over a year. But, after everything that he did to me and Paul, and others, over the years, he risked his life to save Paul that night. Why would he do that? Why torment someone for all that time and then jump into the river to save them? It keeps coming back to me, and I can't get my head around it. He ended up in hospital with a shattered leg, and he's not going to ever be able to walk as well as he did before, never mind run or do the sports that he used to. He made our lives hell, and then tried to rescue Paul. And all for nothing because Paul had got on to the riverbank by himself anyway. It's almost farcical."

"But he didn't know that at the time."

"No. That's true. But there is a certain irony, all the same."

James and his counsellor sat in silence for a few seconds. James couldn't think of anything more to say. The subject had been discussed at previous sessions, and he still hadn't been able to come to terms with the events of that night, and he struggled with things that didn't make sense to him.

"This is our last session, James. Next week you're

off to university. Is there anything else you want to bring up before we finish?"

James shook his head.

"I don't think so. I mean, I'm nervous about going. About leaving Paul behind. Whether I'll cope on my own. Whether *he'll* cope on his own. Whether we'll be able to stay in a long-distance relationship. But you know all of that already. We've talked about it for weeks. I feel it's time to move on. From school. From this town. I'm looking forward to that. To putting the past behind me. Or trying to. I have to do it. I feel like it's a case of now or never. Now or I'll go completely mad, even. I need to *escape*."

"How difficult do you think that might be? To escape. Honestly."

"I have no idea. But it's probably going to be easier for me than it is for Jason. I haven't got a bad leg to remind me of my past, like he has."

"You have memories."

"Yes, and nightmares. Even a scar or two. Another reason why I can't just forget."

"Two years isn't such a long time in which to forget, James. Not for someone who went through what you did."

"I guess I'm frustrated. I don't want to be defined by what happened to me when I was at school. From that point of view, me and Jason are in the same situation."

"You seem more concerned for Jason than you do for yourself."

"No. Not really. It's just that I happened to bump into him, and it took me by surprise."

James sat back in the chair and closed his eyes, taking a few moment to get his thoughts together.

"But I don't like...I don't like the fact that sometimes I feel sorry for him," he went on. "It bothers me. I don't think I should be feeling that. But I guess I've come to realise that things aren't as straightforward as I thought they were. The most difficult thing at the moment is trying to get my head around the idea that nothing is black and white. I'm with Paul, a good guy who did some awful things to me during that last year at school. And then there's Jason, who I always thought was the spawn of the devil, and yet risked his own neck to try and save Paul – whose life he had made a misery for a year. A good guy that does bad things. A bad guy that does good things. It just screws with my head sometimes. I struggle with that idea almost more than anything else."

James glanced at the clock on the table.

"Time's up," he said.

CHAPTER TWO

1

James Marsh gently woke the boy lying next to him.

"You're going to have to move, Paul. I've got a dead arm."

Paul Baker groaned and turned over in bed so that James could move the arm that Paul's head had been resting on. He hated being woken up early in the morning, but today was even worse. It was the day that he had been dreading for months, and he had barely slept all night through thinking about it.

Paul had been living with James and his family ever since he had escaped from his fall in to the river. It had been a temporary, unofficial arrangement to start with, but Paul's parents hadn't seemed to care about what he did or where he stayed.

When his dad died suddenly a few months after Paul had left school, he had gone home to live with his mum, who had moved back into the house with her current boyfriend. It had been a disaster. The boyfriend was no better than his dad had been, and so, when that hadn't worked out, the Marsh family had taken Paul in permanently. It had been inevitable. It felt right.

The two years that followed had been the happiest of Paul's life. For the first time, he had felt wanted and accepted, and part of a real family. He had chipped in towards his keep once he had got a job, and the constant fear that he had suffered while living with his parents had evaporated.

And now, all of that was about to change.

This had been James and Paul's last night together for what could be three months. James was leaving for university later that day.

While James had gone on to sixth form, Paul had found himself a job in a local supermarket. He knew that James had plans to go to university, and would never have tried to stop him – no matter how much he might have liked to. He'd saved as much money as he could over the previous year and had already found himself a small rented bedsit which he would move into over the coming weekend.

James's mum had told Paul he could still live with her, but he didn't want to. It would remind him constantly that James was no longer around, and that their days as a couple might be numbered. Besides, James's family had already done enough. They had looked after him when nobody else had wanted to, and now he needed to try and stand on his own two feet. What he didn't realise was that James's mum viewed him as one of her own family, and could have done with the company now that she was going to be alone in the house with both her children at university.

James snuggled up to Paul, put his arm over his boyfriend's chest and gently kissed his neck.

"I need to get up in a minute," he said. "You can stay in bed if you want to."

"No. We've only got a couple of hours left together. We might as well make the most of it."

James laughed.

"I thought we did that last night."

"You know what I mean."

James kissed Paul again.

"I'm not going to the other side of the world, you know? You can visit. And I'm coming back."

"Yeah, I know, I know. But will you be coming back as my boyfriend?"

James propped himself up on his elbow.

"That again. We've been through this. What makes you keep thinking that I won't?"

Paul turned towards him. He had tried to explain his fears to James before, but they hadn't been taken seriously, and he was told he was worrying unnecessarily.

"You're going to university," he said. "Things are going to be different for you. You're going to meet new people, new friends. New *gay* friends. Ones that you might want to go out with more than me. I'm virtually the only gay person you know, James. You might find someone you like a lot more. It's only natural."

"Don't say that. It won't happen."

"It's true."

And James knew it was.

He was off to university, and realised that things were unlikely to ever be quite the same again. Things *were* going to change. He knew couples a year older than himself where they had gone to different universities, and they had pledged to make a go of it long distance, but it never worked out. Skype helped, of course, but even with a call each night it couldn't make up for seeing each other. Skype was for staying in touch, not for keeping a relationship going.

James hoped that he and Paul would be different, that their relationship would beat the odds, that they would somehow find a way, but he knew deep down that it wasn't very likely. And it wasn't just to do with not being with each other as much. He thought he could trust himself around other guys, but he didn't know about Paul. Despite the fact they had been a couple for the last two years, he hadn't forgotten how Paul had betrayed him in the past.

When they had been at school, James and Paul had been caught kissing by Jason Mitchell and his friends, and Paul had turned on James to save himself from the bullying – not once, but twice. James knew why it had happened, and even understood why Paul did it, but there was always that nagging feeling that it might happen again. He didn't think Paul would cheat on him, but he just couldn't be sure. There was that fear there would be a third betrayal.

James kissed Paul on the lips.

"We'll still be together when I come home at Christmas. I promise."

"I hope so."

"I *know* so. But now I need to shower."

Paul watched as James got out of bed, and padded naked across the bedroom, picking up his towel and wrapping it around his waist.

"I hope you're right about us still being together at Christmas," Paul said. "I don't want this to be the last time I see you with no clothes on."

James smiled at him.

"It won't be," he said. "I'll flash at you when I come back from the shower, too."

James walked out of the room and Paul listened to his footsteps as he walked along the landing to the bathroom. He turned over and lay on his back, staring up the ceiling.

He really didn't think that they could get through such an upheaval as this unscarred, and he even wondered if James was in the right frame of mind to try. Six months of counselling hadn't stopped him from having nightmares and panic attacks on a regular basis. Paul only hoped that going to university would help James rather than make him worse.

2

Since Jonathan's Lewis's newspaper article about the failings at Smithdale Academy had been published two years earlier, many changes had been made at the school.

The Head had lasted just one more day in his job before realizing that there was no way he could do anything but resign over the allegations that he had turned a blind eye to the bullying of James and Paul, and that he had allowed a student to get away with bringing a knife to school. A number of other teachers who had been implicated had also left.

Andrew Green, Jonathan's boyfriend, who thought he would be treated as a pariah for his part in taking the Smithdale Academy story to the newspapers, had been approached by the new headteacher and asked to take back his resignation. He agreed, returning as the acting head of the department before his new position was finalized a few months later after a recruitment process for the job that nobody else was ever going to win. His fellow teachers (those that hadn't resigned) were pleased for him.

But it had been a difficult period, and being a local celebrity was not something Andrew had found easy. He couldn't wait for the attention to go away, but, by the time the story had died down at the end of the summer, it was time for the new school year to begin and he had to put up with yet more attention from both parents and pupils alike as they saw him for the first time since the newspaper article had been printed.

Now, two years on, Andrew sat in front of his first class of the day and stared at them. Not *at* them exactly, but through them. He felt as if he was separated from them in some way, like he was in a glass booth within the classroom, but one where the walls were built with invisible materials. And yet, despite this feeling of distance, Andrew could sense the unease coming from the twenty or so children that sat in front of him. It was palpable. It was only their third week at the school, and now they were faced with a teacher who was out of control.

They didn't speak, but many turned to each other, unsure of what to do. They hadn't ever sat in a lesson with a spaced-out, incoherent teacher before. Oddly, none of them appeared to find the situation amusing. There was no giggling, no joking, no messing around. This was a new experience for them and they found it to be unsettling instead of an opportunity to misbehave. An hour discussing the short story they had read for homework suddenly seemed an attractive proposition. Hell, even writing an essay would be better than this.

Beyond the haze which surrounded him, Andrew Green was well aware that he was losing it. Perhaps it was more than that; he had *already* lost it. No matter how much he wanted to, he couldn't snap himself out of his dazed state. He felt concussed. He felt exhausted – so exhausted that he just couldn't muster the energy to even open his mouth and find the words to apologise to his class, or explain that he was feeling unwell.

He knew that his current state might have been caused by his new medication, but he also knew that this was partly his own fault. Andrew had let things go too far.

The point of no return.

He had been like this before, even if it had been a long time ago, back when he was barely out of his teens. He knew the warning signs from back then, and knew he had ignored them for months before going to the doctors. Why had he left it so long? He had no idea. Sorting it just seemed like more effort than letting it get worse, and now here he was, unable to function at all, and the tablets that might eventually make him better were giving him side effects he could do without.

Not only was he spaced out, but he also felt sick and his stomach sometimes churned so much that he felt as if it was inhabited by a washing machine. He wondered if he would throw up in front of the class. The ultimate humiliation.

He hadn't been surprised that his ill-health had returned. There had been too much pressure. He couldn't live up to the image that had been painted of him after the newspaper story had come out.

He was no hero, despite what had been written about him. He had simply done what was needed to be done, and the stress of those months and the pressure to perform afterwards, to live up to his new reputation, had left him ill and worn out. Now he felt like one of the walking dead.

With the children staring at him, partly in horror,

partly in disbelief, Andrew knew he just had to get out of the classroom. He took a long deep breath, and then finally summoned up enough energy to lean forward in his chair and slowly closed the book in front of him. All eyes followed his every move, wondering why it was that their teacher was moving almost in slow motion, and watching intently to see what he would do next.

He muttered "I'm sorry", and then he stood up and slowly and deliberately put on his jacket. Picking up his briefcase, he forced the slightest of smiles at those in front of him, and then slowly walked out of his classroom.

He wondered if he would ever return.

3

Alfred McKechnie looked up as he heard the shop door open and smiled as James walked in, pulling a suitcase behind him. Alfred put down his ever-present book of Sherlock Holmes stories and slowly got up off his stool to greet him.

"James! I didn't think I'd see you again before you go."

James grinned.

"I didn't want to leave without saying goodbye, Alfred."

James had been going to the shop for years, ever since his uncle had got him interested in old films. He and Alfred, the shop's owner, had struck up a rather unique friendship from the outset, and they had only got closer as time went on. Now the bond between them had become unbreakable, and it was not exaggeration to say they were like grandfather and grandson.

The shop mostly sold mostly a mix of film memorabilia, and records and CDs, and a few shelves of vintage books, mostly green Penguin paperback editions of old crime novels, which James had started reading on quiet days as he sat behind the counter waiting for a customer.

James had been working in the shop part-time for a couple of years, and while Alfred had been saddened when he had told him that their working arrangement had to come to an end because he was going to university, he was pleased for him all the same. Alfred knew how hard James had worked to obtain the grades he needed to get himself on to one of the best film courses in the country, and how difficult it had been for him to get his life back on track after what had happened to him two years earlier.

"Do you have time for a cup of tea, Jim?"

James shook his head.

"I'm sorry, Alfred. My train leaves in half an hour. I just wanted to pop in and say goodbye. And to say thanks for everything. I don't know what I'd have done without you."

The old man smiled, and put his hands on James's shoulders.

"The feeling is mutual, my friend," he said.

"Have you found someone to take my place? Someone to help you on Saturdays?"

Alfred shook his head.

"No, not yet."

Both of them secretly knew that Alfred would never even look for a replacement. The bond between them was special. Nothing and no-one could replace that.

Alfred didn't really need help on a Saturday anyway; the shop rarely had more than one customer in it at a time. A sign of the times. It didn't make enough money to warrant an extra pair of hands even for one day a week, but he had simply enjoyed spending time with James. But now that was coming to an end, and he was no longer sure that he wanted to keep the shop open anymore. He was old. And tired. Dragging himself in to work six days a week was getting too much for him. More importantly, times were changing. His kind of shop was old-fashioned. James had encouraged him to start listing some of the more expensive items in the shop online, so that Alfred got a better price and turnover of stock. Alfred was stuck in his ways, though, and he was the first to admit it. If he couldn't sell things in person then he didn't want to sell them at all. The interaction with the customer was the most important thing, even if many of his old customers had moved away, or even died. His clientele was mostly elderly, and so it was almost inevitable. The shop was just a paying hobby now, but one that required more energy from Alfred than he had left to give.

The shop's days were numbered unless Alfred

changed the way he did business. They both knew it, but neither had said anything about it. It was a fact they both wanted to ignore.

"I came to bring you a present, Alfred," James said. "I was going to save it for Christmas, but I'd like you to have it now instead."

James pulled a package from his bag, poorly wrapped in brown paper with the edges stuck down with wads of sticky tape. He handed it to Alfred.

"Sorry, I'm not good at wrapping presents. Open it when I've gone."

Alfred patted the parcel gently.

"I will," he said. "Thank you. But I didn't expect a present. You shouldn't have done this. You'll have other things to spend your money on now you're at university. Like beer!"

James laughed.

"I don't know about that, Alfred. I'm not even sure I like it. A couple of pints and I just nod off. You can't spend money if you're asleep."

"Well, that's true," Alfred said. "Perhaps that's why we don't get so many customers these days – they're all asleep!"

James smiled at the weak attempt at humour. He knew that Alfred was trying hard to look cheerful despite James going away.

They said their goodbyes, and then Alfred watched James walk out of the shop for what he feared would be the last time. There was no obvious reason to think that; James would be back at Christmas, after all, and Alfred wasn't going to close the shop that quickly – and yet the thought was in his head and he found it impossible to drive it out.

He waited until James had walked out of sight, and then he shuffled slowly back to the counter and started to pick with his arthritic fingers at the sellotape that was plastered on to the brown paper of the parcel. Finally, he gave up and broke into the package with a pair of scissors. He tore away at the paper and then looked down in awe at what sat in front of him: a bound volume of original Strand magazines, the publication in which Alfred's beloved Sherlock Holmes had first appeared.

Alfred settled back into his chair, with the volume resting on his lap. As he browsed through the pages, he realised he was already missing the young man whom he cared for more than his own family. He knew that all things had to come to an end, but for Alfred it seemed that this was more than just a working arrangement coming to a conclusion. At some point in the near future, he would hang the "closed" sign on the front door of the shop for the last time. This was the start of the last chapter. He also knew that his health was getting worse – nothing specific, but everything just seemed to be slowing down.

He turned another page of the book and found himself looking at the Sherlock Holmes story called *His Last Bow*.

Alfred smiled at the irony.

As soon as Jonathan Lewis walked in through the front door of the house he shared with his boyfriend, he knew that something was wrong.

It was more than just instinct or a gut feeling. Normally there would be the sound coming from the kitchen of dinner being made, often accompanied by a string of swear words and some loud jazz from the CD player. Andrew liked both jazz and swearing. Tonight, there was nothing. No sound at all.

But it wasn't just the quietness. There was almost a palpable air of unease hanging over the house, something he couldn't quite put his finger on. No lights were on, and yet there was no note on the fridge telling him that his other half had nipped out to the shop and would be back in five minutes. He knew that he could have just been delayed at work or something like that, but his gut told him that it was something more and, as a journalist, Jonathan knew that gut instinct was normally the thing you should trust most.

He went to the bottom of the stairs and shouted up them.

"Andrew?"

No sound came from upstairs, but he ran up the stairs anyway. The bathroom door was wide open, but he was sure he had shut it that morning before leaving for work. So, Andrew must have come home at some point during the day. Jonathan walked slowly along the hallway, pushed open the bedroom door and switched on the light.

He was relieved to see Andrew lying in the bed, fully-clothed and wrapped tightly within the duvet. But something wasn't right. Jonathan sat down on the edge of the bed and gently woke him up. Andrew groaned and turned over to face him.

"Hey, Mr. Sleepy," Jonathan said.

"Hi," came the somber, barely audible, reply.

"What's all this about? You coming down with something?"

Andrew shook his head.

"No. Just tired."

Jonathan knew there was more to it than that. In their two years together, he had learned to tell when Andrew was only half telling the truth. And there had been lots of occasions when that had happened, especially when Andrew had tried to give up alcohol and failed, but tried to hide it. And Jonathan had realised long after the event that, when he had asked Andrew if he was sure about the newspaper running the story he had written about the school, Andrew was only half telling the truth when he had said "yes." What he had meant was "yes, I want them to run it, but I'm not sure I'm strong enough to deal with the consequences." Jonathan feared that this was yet another one of those consequences. They had been piling up for some time.

"Just tired?" he asked. "Are you sure?"

Andrew nodded his head and forced a smile. Then shook his head and sank back into the pillows as if the weight of his head was too much for his body to carry.

"I've had enough," Andrew said. "I'm done."

"What do you mean?"

Andrew stared up at the ceiling.

"This morning. I just cracked," he said, speaking slower than usual. "I was sitting there in the classroom first period, with the kids in front of me. I was all ready to teach. All ready to try and get enthusiastic about some stupid story I'd made them read for homework. But then suddenly it was as if I wasn't really there. Almost as if I was looking at them through frosted glass. I was there, but I couldn't do anything. I didn't have the energy or the focus, I guess, to even tell them to sit there and read quietly. I was just…someplace else. And it wasn't a *nice* place, Jon. I was incapable of doing anything. It was so weird. Scary. These bloody new tablets are making me feel like shit, as well."

He closed his eyes.

"I just want to stay in bed forever," he said. "You don't mind if I do that, do you?"

It wasn't as if Jonathan hadn't realised that this moment was coming. In fact, he had encouraged Andrew to go on sick leave a week or so earlier, but he had refused. It was the start of term and he was head of the department. He needed to be there.

"What happened at the school?" Jonathan asked.

"I don't know. Panic attack or something I guess. The same old thing."

"No, I meant, what did you do?"

"I just eventually got up and left them. I just walked out of the classroom, out of the school and came home.

I left them there unsupervised."

"I'm sure they coped, Andrew. One of them would have got a teacher. They're kids, but they're not stupid."

"They were year sevens. They've only been at the school three weeks, and now they've had a teacher go ga-ga on them. The school's been ringing up all afternoon. There's messages on the answer phone. I just couldn't talk to them. Didn't have the energy."

"I'll go in and talk to them tomorrow. They'll understand. But first you're going back to the doctors. And it's my day off, so I'm coming with you."

"There'll never be an appointment. You have to wait weeks. You know what it's like these days."

"I'll make sure you get seen. I can be very persuasive – even with that old dragon in reception. We'll get you back on your feet in no time." He forced a smile. "What do you say I nip out and get a takeaway? You can get up and have a shower or something while I'm gone. It'll make you feel a bit more alive."

"I'm not hungry."

"I realise that, but you're going to eat or you'll feel even worse."

Jonathan got up off the bed and held out his hand to his boyfriend.

"Come on you, out of that bed."

Andrew looked at him for a few seconds and then grabbed his hand and allowed himself to be pulled up. His legs felt weak, his body felt sweaty.

"That's better," Jonathan said. "Now, get in the shower while I'm gone. You smell riper than some of the customers in the 99p shop."

"You have such a way with words."

"That's me."

Jonathan was halfway down the hallway when Andrew called after him. He walked back to the bedroom.

"You don't have to stay," Andrew said. "I've been here before. A long time ago. It's not going to be pretty; this isn't going to be nice for you. You don't need this. You can just get your stuff together while I'm in the shower, get in the car, and go. I won't hold it against you."

Jonathan knew that Andrew was right. This wasn't going to be a fun ride, but there was no chance that he was going to walk away.

"Neither of us need this. But you need me, and I need you. The only place I'm going is to the takeaway," he said. "I'll be back in twenty minutes."

5

James sat on the train, waiting for it to leave the platform. It had already seemed like a long day and yet it was only mid-morning.

His mum and Paul had wanted to go to the station to see him off, but he had told them firmly that he didn't want them to. Both had cried like babies when he left the house that morning, and he didn't think he would have been able to cope with it at the station. He remembered all too well the scene beside the train when Rachel had left for university two years earlier. His Mum had been virtually inconsolable, and so the thought of her putting in a repeat performance with Paul bawling beside her was not an attractive one. No, this was much better. He would only end up feeling guilty for going if he had seen them so upset, and this was one thing he didn't want to feel bad about. Going to university was going to be traumatic enough.

He had nerves, plenty of them. And he was worried about leaving Paul, his mum and Alfred, but he knew that this was something he had to do – he had to finally escape the memories of the horrible time that he had endured a couple of years earlier.

Those events had been invading his dreams and his thoughts more and more in recent weeks. More than once he had woken up beside Paul, screaming and sweating. He had told him that he couldn't remember the dreams that had frightened him so much, but he often could. Each and every one he could recall was a warped, slightly surreal re-enactment of a bullying incident he had gone through at the hands of Jason Mitchell and his friends. And Paul's betrayal was part of them. He hoped that a new start in a new place would help him escape those old memories, although he was far from convinced.

He had struggled on to the train with his suitcase, but now it was safely wedged in the luggage rack at the far end of the carriage, although he had no idea how he was going to get it out again. When he found a seat, he slowly thumbed through the pages of the latest issue of *Sight and Sound* that he had bought at the station while he was waiting for the train to be ready to board. He turned to the film review section. Cinema tickets were cheaper as a student, so he hoped he might get to see more movies while he was at uni.

He looked out of the window as the train started to pull away from the station. His journey was only going to take a couple of hours, but to James it was like he was moving a million miles away. He turned back to his magazine and flicked through it again, this time trying to concentrate on an article about a recent restoration of a group of early films, but, in the end, he just gave up, rested his head on the window and watched the scenery go by.

Two hours later, James was awoken by a man gently nudging him.

"I think this might be your station, young man?" the man said.

James opened his eyes and looked out of the window.

"Shit. Yes. Thanks."

He smiled at the man and then hurried down the carriage where he finally managed to wrench his suitcase out of the luggage rack before stepping off the train.

The information he had received from the university told him that he could catch a bus outside the station and it would take him directly to campus, but he felt he couldn't be bothered with lumping his suitcase on and off the bus and then getting lost when he got to campus, and so he made his way to the taxi rank. If the bus journey really was only a fifteen-minute ride, then the same trip in a cab was hardly going to eat up all of his student loan. Not that he had got it yet.

The cab driver wound down the window as James approached, and James told him he was heading for the university.

"Will be about eight quid," James was told.

"That's fine," he replied, and got in after the driver had put his suitcase in the boot.

"Is this your first year here?" the taxi driver asked as they pulled out of the station car park.

"Yes," James replied. "I came to look around a few months back, but that's the only time I've been here."

"You'll like it. Everyone does. Not many students go back home when they've finished their three years. They all want to stay here because they like it so much. Of course, you have to go where the work is these days, though."

The driver chatted away, mostly pointing out places of interest, and, fifteen minutes later, James arrived on campus. He paid and thanked the driver and then looked around in the hope that there might be a sign to the office where he could pick up the keys for his room. He didn't find one, but a couple of people gave him directions and about half an hour later he finally reached his accommodation block.

It was with some trepidation that he put the key in

the lock and opened the door. He walked in, dragging his suitcase behind him. It was a little bigger than he expected – he knew his sister's room at university had been tiny. However, his was in what seemed to be a relatively new building. It still wasn't as big as his bedroom back home, but it wasn't too small, and it was clean. He opened the door to the bathroom and saw that it was so small that he would be able to have the novelty of sitting on the toilet and washing his feet in the shower at the same time if he wanted. His wardrobe at home was bigger than the bathroom, but at least he didn't have to face the embarrassment of communal showers. He wouldn't have been able to cope with that. It would have been like being back at school, and school was one place he didn't want to be reminded of.

CHAPTER THREE

1

Jonathan Lewis pulled the car to a halt outside the house he had shared with Andrew Green for over a year. He turned off the engine, and sat back in his seat, not really sure what to do with the information that he had just been given.

He had intended his visit to the school to be a short one in which he would meet with the headteacher, apologise for Andrew leaving his class the day before, and explain to her what the situation was, and that Andrew sadly wouldn't be back at work for a little while. That part of the conversation went well but, after that, things had not gone quite according to plan.

Mrs. Washburn (a distinct improvement on the previous headteacher, Jonathan thought), had thanked him for coming in and for explaining the situation, but had then said that the school had been concerned with Andrew's behaviour since the middle of the previous term.   She had listed a series of incidents involving Andrew that Jonathan had known nothing about. While he secretly wondered whether she should have been telling him these things due to confidentiality issues, he also realised that, because most of them had happened in front of the kids, they would be common knowledge anyway.

"On more that one occasion, pupils have been overheard by teachers in the corridor discussing Mr. Green's behavior," Mrs. Washburn had said.

"What sort of behavior?"

"Well…" Mrs. Washburn had paused for a second to try to gather her thoughts and make sure she worded her reply as best as she could. "There has certainly been talk about how many expletives Mr. Green had used in class."

"Oh?"

"Yes. In all honesty, I am pretty certain that the pupils mind considerably less than we do, and it's fair to say that anyone can have a lapse and allow a word to slip out occasionally without meaning to. We've all done it, you know?"

Jonathan nodded.

"But he did, according to the story, tell one of his pupils he was a 'fucking pain in the arse.'"

"Shit."

"Yes. Quite. Now, to be honest, Mr. Lewis, bearing in mind the pupil he was referring to, I don't blame him, but that is somewhat beside the point, don't you think?"

"Yes. I had no idea."

"It's obviously not the kind of language we expect in the classroom. Of course, no teachers heard it, and no pupil has formerly reported it. And I very much doubt that they ever will – Mr. Green is liked by most pupils. And, in all honesty, they probably rather like that he has been letting swearwords slip out during lessons. You know how kids are."

Jonathan finished the coffee in front of him.

"Have you spoken to Andrew about this?"

"No. Not yet. But it is going to have to happen at some point if it carries on, you understand? On another occasion, pupils have apparently seen Mr. Green get up from his desk, go into the walk-in cupboard at the back of the room and close the door, returning ten minutes later with it being rather obvious that he had been crying. Again, nothing has been said to us officially, but teachers *have* heard him crying in a stall in the toilets. And this has been after the summer holidays, not before. In all honesty, many of us feel like crying at the end of term, but less so at the beginning."

Perhaps most worrying for Jonathan was that Mrs. Washburn had said that she believed she had smelt alcohol on Andrew's breath one lunchtime, and wondered if his ever-present flask contained something other than coffee:

"I'm not exactly in a position to ask him to prove what he has in his flask, and I can hardly ask him to take a breathalyser, but I am pretty certain that my sense of smell was not deceiving me."

It was clear that something was amiss, and Mrs.

Washburn reiterated to Jonathan that Andrew had to make sure he was completely well before he returned to work.

Jonathan knew that she was being generous in not taking any action, but Andrew had gone through a lot for (and because of) the school, and probably deserved a little bit of leeway. Even so, any more incidents like the ones of recent months and any authority he had over the pupils would be well and truly at an end. Despite the fact that the school was willing to forget these issues for now, or at least set them aside, it was clear that Andrew's position would be in jeopardy if anything similar occurred once he returned to work.

The big question for Jonathan now was what he should do with the information, and it played on his mind as he sat in the car. Should he tell Andrew that he knew things were worse than he had been letting on? Or keep it quiet, hoping that his boyfriend would take some time off, let the tablets do their job, and hopefully make a recovery? He wondered if Andrew even remembered doing the things that Mrs. Washburn had told him about.

Jonathan's knowledge of depression was not great, but he had known others who had lived with people with the condition, and he was well aware that the next few weeks or months (or years) were not going to be easy. One thing was for sure – he needed to hit Google and find out as much as he could about depression. The more he knew about what to expect, the more he thought he would be able to deal with it, and the more he could help Andrew get through it.

"You don't need this," Andrew had told him the night before, and Jonathan knew that was true.

He had spent months helping Andrew kick his drinking habit, and that was difficult enough – although it now appeared that he hadn't kicked it quite as well as Jonathan thought. He wouldn't have minded if Andrew had told him he had been drinking again, but keeping it to himself was something of a kick in the teeth.

Jonathan looked up at the house, dreading the rest of his day off. Not only would he now have to face Andrew knowing what he did, but there was a trip to the doctors later in the afternoon to look forward to – one that he had almost had to beg the receptionist for. She had been intent on giving him an appointment two weeks later, and there was no way that Jonathan was letting Andrew carry on for that long before seeing the doctor again. But she had taken a great deal of persuasion. At least by having an appointment on his day off, Jonathan could go with him and would not have to rely on Andrew's account of what happened, or trust him to tell the doctor how he really felt. It was clear that Andrew could not be believed.

He saw the curtains in the lounge twitch, and realised that Andrew would be standing there and wondering why he hadn't gone indoors.

As he opened the car door, Jonathan made up his mind that he would tell Andrew about what Mrs. Washburn had said to him. If he wanted Andrew to be honest with him, then he had to be honest with Andrew.

At least if they were completely open about the situation, they would know what they were dealing with, and that might help in getting Andrew back on his feet quicker and more successfully.

2

Jason Mitchell walked back to his bedroom, shut the door, pulled at the towel that was wrapped around his waist, letting it drop to the floor, and pulled on a clean pair of boxer shorts. He flopped down on to the bed, having come to the realisation that he was obviously nothing more than a disappointment to his parents.

Half an hour earlier, when he had finished eating dinner, he had asked his mother for fifty pounds. She had sighed, reached into her handbag and, without saying anything, handed him the cash he had asked for. His father had watched on without commenting.

Every time Jason Mitchell asked his parents for money, they gave it to him. No questions were ever asked as to what he might want it for, and no hints were ever given that he should get up off his backside and start looking for a job so that he would have his own money. He felt that they had basically given up on him, and that their current plan was to give him whatever he asked for within reason, in the hope that he would lead a quiet life and not embarrass them and/or get arrested.

To some degree, Jason couldn't blame them. He

had brought on many of his troubles himself. His bullying of James and Paul had, after all, ended up as part of a big local news story a couple of years earlier and brought his family's name into the newspapers in a way that, for once, his father didn't approve of.

His father, Peter, had often been in the newspapers before, beaming away playing the local high-flying businessman who had given another batch of computers away to a local charity or school. But it was all a con; the goods he gave away were worth it for the amount of free publicity he got in return. It was like a pop star issuing a charity single in the hope that people might buy it and then go on to buy the album. Jason had learned that virtually everything Peter Mitchell did was cold and calculated.

Peter had also been implicated in the news story from two years earlier, with it suggested that he had abused his friendship with the head teacher at the school so that Jason wasn't excluded or suspended for his conduct which, as well as bullying, had included the distribution of drugs on the school premises and taking a knife to school. Jason knew that there had been some truth in that, too. Had it not been for his father, he would have been more severely punished in the first place, and things might not have turned out the way they had. Jason was responsible for his own actions, and he knew that - but he also knew that being protected by his parents from the repercussions of those actions for so long had made the whole situation worse. Would he have stopped much earlier if he had been punished?

However, the bullying and other misdeeds that Jason had been behind were far from the biggest disappointment he had dealt to his parents. Instead, that was not being the genius that they had intended him to be. Twenty thousand pounds was still sitting in a bank for him for when he went to university to train to become a doctor or a lawyer or a computer whiz like his father. It had been there since he was seven. His life had been mapped out for him even at that age. But the future his parents wanted for him was never going to happen.

The truth was that Jason didn't have Peter Mitchell's brains, and so studying law or medicine or science at a prestigious university was not actually on the cards. This realization had own dawned on his parents a couple of years earlier, and they had yet to get over their disappointment. Having Jason go to one of the best universities in the country to study something *they* deemed as worthwhile would have been the next status symbol to add to their current collection. As he couldn't help with their plans, he no longer mattered, and his parents let him do pretty much what he wanted, when he wanted, and gave him money as and when he asked for it, providing he stayed out of trouble and didn't cause any more embarrassment to the family.

That was the term they had used when he had come out of hospital following the attempt to save Paul from drowning and everything had finally died down after the newspaper stories: "we don't want you to be an embarrassment to the family." There was no dressing down for his conduct, or for beating the crap out of a number of other kids, or videoing his bullying and posting it online, or even for taking the knife to school. That didn't matter to the Mitchells. Jason could do what he wanted in that regard as long as he didn't bring shame on the family name. He had begun to wonder if that was the family's motto.

Jason might not have been the brains of the family, but he could still draw. And he knew he was good at it. He had been pleading for the last six months to be allowed to go to the local college to take a course so that he could do an art degree later on, but the answer was "no," and it was given with no explanation as to why it would not be the right thing for him to do.

He had done everything he could to make his parents change their mind. He had shown them his artwork, but they had not been interested. He had stayed out of trouble, and done his best to find a job after leaving school. When he wasn't even able to get a job at the local supermarket, he finally realised that it was probably due to the newspaper stories. He wondered how long he would have to pay for his past behaviour.

He had changed, or tried his best to, but nobody would believe him. He had apologised to James and Paul a year ago. Too little too late, he knew, but at least he had made the effort.

He had then spent much of the last year hanging around the art department at the college, talking to students there, even some of the staff. One female student he had got to know a little bit had even asked him to model for her so that she could draw him. The Jason of two years earlier would have taken that in his stride and even been big-headed about it, but he had been genuinely flattered, despite the fact that he was well aware of how good-looking he was. Plus, Madeline was cute, and she knew nothing about the old Jason.

Finally, one of the teachers at the college looked at Jason's work. He told him about his situation, and how his parents wouldn't pay for him to study what he wanted, despite their wealth. The teacher encouraged him to put his work into a competition for a scholarship that would pay the tuition fees of the winner. He had come third, meaning 50% of his fees would be covered. Jason took the offer, not knowing where the remainder of the money would come from, but he didn't care. He would find a way. He just wanted the chance to show people who he really was and what he could really do. Surely everyone deserved a second chance? He still hadn't told his parents, despite starting classes the week before. They didn't even seem to notice that he was busier than normal and out of the house more often.

He'd made new friends too. Rick had been at the college a year already and his brother, Mark, had started at the same time as Jason. He'd been introduced to Rick by Madeline, the girl he had modelled for. She had woven something of a spell over Jason, who was amused by the way someone as pretty as her could also be cocky and fun. Madeline was really quite different to any girl he had met before, with the possible exception of Jane, who had been part of his circle of friends at school.

New friends and a new start. Jason was feeling proud of himself, and, for the first time in a long while, he knew he had every reason to be.

Jason glanced at the clock and realised he had been lying down for half an hour. He got up off the bed, took a pair of jeans out of the wardrobe and pulled them on. He picked up the money his mother had given him earlier and shoved it in his pocket.

Just a couple of hours, and then he would be going out. Poker was his new way of spending Friday nights. He hadn't really known how to play when Rick had first invited him a couple of months back, but he had soon picked it up and was surprised at how good he was at it. It was normally just the four of them: Rick, Mark, Madeline and Jason. Sometimes one of them invited another friend to join them, but Jason preferred it when it was just the four of them as, it would be tonight. His new friends had yet to learn that the money he bought the drinks and gambled with came from his parents. In fact, they knew nothing about his family or his past, and that was just the way he liked it. There was no reason for them to know about who he used to be, and he knew it could be the end of their friendship if they ever did. He wouldn't know how to face them.

Jason had still needed to find a way to pay for the rest of his college fees, and he had run out of obvious options. Slowly, however. he was building a pot of money for the tuition, but not in a way he wanted to or was proud of.

He went over to his laptop, lifted up the lid and switched it on. As it booted up, he slipped into a shirt, leaving it partly undone, and then sat down at his computer desk. He opened his web browser and clicked on one of his bookmarked websites. He signed into it, and then changed his status to "Tips welcome, raising money for college. No private shows."

He made sure that his webcam was in such a position that it only showed him from the neck down, and then he clicked on the "broadcast" button. He would be devastated if anyone found out what he was doing, and so hiding his face was essential. He knew it was still a risk – someone might identify him by his tattoo, for example – but he knew that the chances were very small.

A few minutes after going online, he received a message asking him how many tokens he wanted to take his shirt off. Tokens could be exchanged for cash, which would be deposited in his bank account whenever he decided to withdraw it.

He slowly unbuttoned his shirt and took it off, gaining fifty tokens for his effort and therefore making himself five pounds richer. The same person paid another fifty for him to take off his jeans.

As he sat there in just his boxer shorts, the number of people watching him rose to nearly one hundred. The number of tokens rose quickly as various people donated to the fund and, when it reached one hundred, he stood up and pulled down his boxers. He had got naked in front of one hundred people for £20.

He had earned another £30 by the time he switched off the webcam an hour later. He grabbed some tissues from the box on his desk to clean himself up with. Another £50 in total towards his college tuition, and, as time went on, Jason was becoming less and less bothered by how he was raising it.

3

"Twenty minutes late. What's the bloody hold up?"

"You won't be upset if she takes longer than ten minutes with you, so stop moaning when she runs over with other patients."

Andrew and Jonathan had been sitting in the doctor's waiting room for nearly half an hour, having arrived ten minutes early. They waited, subconsciously huddle together as they avoided the germs of others in the same area.

One man had been sneezing and coughing ever since he had arrived, and had somehow reached what appeared to be late middle-age without learning the art of sneezing into a tissue or putting his hand across his mouth when he coughed. Luckily, Andrew and Jonathan were on the opposite side of the room, but they still wondered how far such germs could travel.

A woman a few seats down had made at least three visits to the toilets since she had come into the waiting room ten minutes earlier, making everyone else feel (rightly or wrongly) that they were going to catch an horrendous stomach bug and that they should make a mental note to buy some Imodium on the way home. Elsewhere, there was the usual assortment of injured limbs, severe nosebleeds, crying babies, and people with no visible sign of illness.

Like Andrew.

The wait had been uncomfortable and tense, with Andrew still in a mood from hearing what Mrs. Washburn had told Jonathan.

"She had no right to tell you that," he had said.

Jonathan suggested that her breaking confidentiality was hardly the point. While he suspected that Andrew didn't even remember some of the occurrences, he was very sure that he remembered the fact that he was drinking again, and this had pissed Jonathan off. In the end, though, he knew that it was all linked to Andrew's depression and so would do his best to take things one step at a time: get his boyfriend some medication that actually did some good and then work on the alcohol issue. Andrew, on the other hand, wasn't being quite so pragmatic. He was sulking, and Jonathan knew that it was likely to last all day, and that was something he could do without.

They both looked up as another patient walked out of the corridor that housed the doctors' offices, and hoped that they would be called next. A buzzer accompanied the name of another patient appearing on the screen above the receptionist's window, and Andrew grumbled to himself and picked up a copy of

Woman's Own from the table.

It was another twenty minutes before he was finally seen. Andrew wanted to go in alone, but Jonathan was having none of it, and there was no changing his mind. He wanted to know what was going on, as this was going to affect him as much as Andrew. What was more, he didn't trust Andrew to truthfully relay the conversation to him afterwards.

"Nice to see you again, Mr. Green," the doctor said as they walked into the office.

Andrew forced a smile while secretly thinking that it was a stupid thing for a doctor to say. He sat down and explained what had happened.

"So, the Fluoxetine has not produced any positive results, then?" the doctor asked.

"It has produced results like having the runs and feeling sick," Andrew replied, with little attempt to hide his dwindling patience.

"You started on them three weeks ago. That's right, isn't it?"

Andrew nodded.

"I think I'm worse rather than better," he said. "In fact, I know I'm worse rather than better. I was at least functioning before. Now I can't even teach. I'm like a zombie sometimes."

"He's been acting out of character at work as well," Jonathan chipped in. Andrew stared at him. "If you don't tell her, she won't know," he added.

"Well," the doctor said, "it seems a bit early to give up on the Fluoxetine just yet. I think the way forward is to try them for another couple of weeks while increasing the dose to see if that helps."

Andrew slumped in his chair.

"But they make me feel like shit. I feel sick, and all I want to do is sleep."

"Those side effects should wear off in time."

"When?"

"That depends from person to person, Mr. Green. Some people don't even have any side effects."

"Lucky them. And how am I meant to feel better if I constantly think I am about to chuck up?"

As Jonathan watched the pair talk, he began to realise that choosing the right doctor for the right ailment and the right patient was key, and that it hadn't happened here. While Andrew was sulking like a kid who wasn't getting his own way, the doctor wasn't exactly sympathetic either, and she wasn't listening to her patient.

While Andrew hadn't said it in as many words, it was quite clear that he wasn't happy with his current medication and wanted an alternative. However, that message wasn't getting through, although it wasn't as if Andrew was being unclear. Jonathan wondered if he should speak up and suggest changing the tablets. He couldn't see how there would be an improvement if Andrew didn't trust the medication to start with.

"I also think counselling would be a good idea," the doctor said.

Jonathan expected Andrew to object, but he didn't. He just nodded and agreed with the doctor to increase the dose of his tablets.

"I shall refer you for some counselling," the doctor went on.

"OK. And when should I hear about that?"

"The waiting list is quite long."

"How long."

"Around a year on the NHS."

"A *year*?" Jonathan said, incredulously. "How is that possible?"

"I'm sorry," the doctor said. "You may have an assessment as quickly as a few days, but, after that, it's a long wait, I'm afraid. Unless you are suicidal or having suicidal thoughts, I can't do anything to speed up the time on the waiting list. You're not having suicidal thoughts, I presume?"

"Not yet."

"Surely the idea is to have counselling to *prevent* him getting to that stage?" Jonathan asked. "What happened to all this talk of parity between physical and mental health?"

"Ask the health secretary," the doctor replied. "I'm sorry. It's out of my hands. I can provide you with the contact details of some counselling centres in the area that provide talking therapies at reduced rates – charitable organisations in the main – if that is of any use to you?"

"OK. Thanks. We can take a look."

The doctor opened a drawer and pulled out a couple of leaflets, giving one each to Andrew and Jonathan.

"I'll see you in a month," she said as they left the room.

Jonathan looked at his watch as they walked down the corridor. In and out in seven minutes. So much for talking your problems over with a doctor. The appointment had been almost a tweet.

He wondered how many others with depression or other mental health conditions were dealt with in the same way. Andrew was lucky, Jonathan was there to make sure he was OK, no matter how difficult it (or he) might be. But what about people who lived on their own? People in a worse state than Andrew? Did they just get turfed out of the appointment in a few minutes with a prescription in their hands and a year-long wait for the treatment they needed?

Jonathan knew that suicide was one of the biggest killers of young men in the country. He had written about it in the newspaper, and wondered what outcry there would be if cancer sufferers were told to wait a year for the treatment they needed.

The journey home was surprisingly quiet, especially as Jonathan had expected a fair amount of moaning about the doctor and the fact he was coming home with the same medication he had gone with. It was only as they neared the house that Andrew said what Jonathan had been expecting to hear since they had left the doctors.

"She can arrange an appointment with a counsellor if she wants, but I'm not going to see some woman in a Laura Ashley dress who sits there nodding at everything

I say like a bloody toy dog in the back of someone's car."

Each and every time Jonathan had brought up the subject of counselling in the past, Andrew referred back to the counsellor he had seen last time he was depressed. Jonathan had tried to explain to him that not all counsellors were the same, and that there were different types of counselling, but Andrew wouldn't hear of it. As if it would matter anyway – a year-long waiting list would mean that Andrew would hopefully be better and back at work by the time he saw someone.

When Jonathan pulled up outside the house, he turned to Andrew and said:

"You're ill and you feel like shit. I understand that. I will help you through it, you know I will. But your feeling crap isn't any excuse for acting like a spoilt teenager."

With that, Jonathan got out of the car and slammed the car door shut, and the two men didn't speak to each other for the rest of the evening.

4

"So, Madeline hasn't got you doing any more nude modelling then?" Rick asked as he dealt the cards, winking at Madeline as he did so.

Jason felt himself blush.

"It wasn't nude modelling," he said.

"I bet Maddy wishes it was," chipped in Mark.

Despite being brothers, Rick and Mark weren't much alike. Rick was tall and slim with blonde hair. He was charming, courteous and witty. Mark, on the other hand, was shorter and stockier, built like a rugby player. His hair was a mass of tight brown curls, and he had little of the sharp humour of his brother, despite the fact he tried endlessly to match his wit. Mark's attempts more often than not came over as crude, not that Jason had a problem with that.

The brothers sat opposite each other at the table, with Madeline facing Jason. He didn't have a problem with that either. He was quite happy to be where he could see her as much as possible. He was sure that it was her smile that was putting him off the game and making him lose.

"I can confirm that neither of us were naked," Madeline said. "Although if Jason loses any more of his chips tonight he might be forced into betting his clothes instead. What do you reckon?"

She smiled, and slowly rubbed her foot up his calf underneath the table. It was all Jason could do to keep from laughing.

"Nah, don't think so," he said. "If I lose these I'll call it a night."

"Shame."

"I'm sure Jason would play strip poker with you any night of the week, Maddy," Mark said. "I'd just rather not watch, if that's all the same. Well, not if he loses anyway. You losing would be alright, though."

"Well, thank you for the compliment," Madeline

replied. "But don't get your hopes up, Mark. The chances of me getting naked in front of you is very slim."

The chances of Jason winning the hand were slim, too. A jack and a six were unlikely to be a winning combination, especially how his luck had been all night. But he realised he might as well play the hand anyway. The blinds would be going up in a hand or two, and he would be out of chips when it was time for him to post the big blind. Jason moved his few remaining chips into the middle of the table.

"All in."

Mark looked at him.

"That's not a confident face I see before me," he said.

"I've not had a good night."

"We can see that, but I fold."

Madeline smiled again across the table at Jason.

"I'll call, of course," she said, and dropped her chips on top of Jason's.

Rick put down his cards.

"Fold," he said, "I'll let you two lovebirds thrash this one out," he said.

Jason looked across at him. While he didn't mind the occasionally joke, he didn't like the constant insinuations, not least because he *was* genuinely interested in Madeline and he was oddly embarrassed about it, although he couldn't work out why.

"We are not lovebirds," he said. "We've never been out. Never kissed. Never done anything."

"Yeah, yeah," Mark said, and finished his can of

beer, burping loudly afterwards.

"Well, you can tell why I never went out with *you*," Madeline said to him.

"I'm a gentleman."

"Riiiiight. Jason might stand a chance one day, though," she said to him.

"Is that so?" Jason responded.

"You won't know till you ask."

Jason won the hand with three sixes, but was still out of the game ten minutes later. He hung around until the bitter end, though, not least because it gave him the opportunity to give Madeline a lift home, and he wanted to find out if he really did stand a chance of going out with her.

He hadn't had a girlfriend for two years, since he broke up with Claire, but that had hardly been a match made in heaven. He may have gone to see James and Paul to apologise for bullying them, but he had never worked up the guts to apologise to his ex-girlfriend face to face for how he had treated her, despite the fact he knew he hurt and, in some ways abused, her. He had written her an email, though, but never got a response. He hadn't expected one, thinking that she would assume the message was a lame attempt to get back with her, and he wasn't wrong. It had only been a few months after they had split up, and Claire had cried lots when she received it, more out of anger than anything else, and then she had trashed it and blocked Jason's email address. She needn't have done, Jason wasn't about to try to contact her again; he had found it hard enough to write the first email.

It was as Jason and Madeline were saying their goodbyes at the front door that Mark said:

"Shit, I nearly forgot to ask. I've got a mate who'd like to join us for the next game. Do either of you mind?"

Jason did mind. Very much. He hated it when extra people came along; he liked the poker nights just as they were. It was never the same when other people were there. But he was also new to the games himself, and knew that he had been welcomed by the others, so he had no real option but to agree.

"Yeah, it's fine by me," he said.

"Nice one," Mark said, and burped again.

"Who is it?" Madeline asked.

"Neil. You know Neil, don't you?"

"Sadly. Quite why you spend time with him, I have no idea. The boy's an idiot."

"Oi!"

"Well, he is. I'm surprised he can even play poker, sometimes I'm not even sure he remembers his own name. But hey, if you want to bring him so you've got someone to belch with, then it's OK by me. But just the once. I can't cope with him every week."

Jason and Madeline got in the car, and a few minutes later, Jason stopped outside Madeline's house.

"Thanks for the lift," she said as she undid her safety belt.

"A pleasure."

She sat in the car, not moving. Jason thought he had

done something wrong. Eventually Madeline said:

"Are you going to ask me, or what?"

"Ask you what?"

"Out for a drink, idiot. I couldn't have given you a bigger hint back there, could I? What do you want, written permission from my dad?"

"Do you think he'd give it?"

"I reckon there's worse guys than you around, Jason Mitchell."

"Thanks. I think. I thought you were just kidding back there about a date."

"No, you didn't. You just didn't have the guts to ask. I can't make you out, Jason. On the one hand you're all cocky and jack-the-lad, and then you're suddenly shy and retiring. I can't work out which is the real you."

"Perhaps they're both me. Which one do you like best?"

Madeline thought for a moment.

"Not sure, I need to get to know them both better first. Eight o'clock tomorrow. Perhaps it will help me decide. Don't be late."

With that she got out of the car and slammed the door shut. Jason watched her as she walked up the path to her house and went inside.

He wouldn't dream of being late.

CHAPTER FOUR

1

James Marsh was awoken by a knocking at the door. Opening his eyes, he quickly tried to remember where he was and what he was doing there. It was only the second morning that he had woken up in his room at university, and the fact that he wasn't in his own bed in his own room at home disoriented him somewhat.

The sun had found a gap where the curtains didn't quite meet and was shining directly into his eyes. He slowly worked out where he was, stretched, and then remembered that the mattress in his room provided none of the comfort that his one at home did. His back was killing him.

He tried to shake off the remnants of his dream. On this occasion, he couldn't remember what it was about, but it hadn't been pleasant, he was sure of that. His dreams had rarely been pleasant for the last few months, but at least up until now he'd had the comfort of waking up next to his boyfriend in the morning, and that helped him forget whatever had troubled him during the night. That wasn't likely to happen again until the Christmas holidays, and it seemed a long time away. It frustrated James that sometimes he could remember his bad dreams, but not always. Paul had told him that he often cried in his sleep, or yelled out as if in pain. Perhaps he was better off sometimes not knowing what was going on in his head when he was asleep.

The knock at the door came again. James swung his legs over the bed, stood up and pulled on a pair of jeans, stumbling across the floor as he did so.

"I'll be there in a sec!" he shouted.

He searched around for a T-shirt and finally found one, and he fought his way into it before opening the door. He needn't have bothered getting fully dressed, for the person who had awoken him hadn't gone to the same amount of trouble.

Standing in front of him was a Greek God in a towel. James didn't know where to look. He tried to look the boy in the face as he said "hi" but wasn't sure that he was totally succeeding as his eyes kept getting distracted by the gym-fit chest and stomach that he knew he could never have the self-discipline to work at. He had never quite figured out where people got that amount of willpower from. The gym seemed far too much like hard work.

"Hi," the Adonis said, "I think I woke you. I'm sorry. I didn't mean to."

"It doesn't matter. I should probably be up

anyway," James said, wiping some sleep from his eyes. "What time is it?"

The stranger brushed his blonde hair away from his eyes with his hand.

"I'm Adam," he said, ignoring James's question and making him think that this wasn't exactly the middle of the morning.

"James."

"Pleased to meet you." They shook hands. "It looks like we're neighbours. I've got the room next door."

"Cool."

James stretched again, hoping his back ache would wear off during the morning. Adam watched him.

"The beds are shit, aren't they?" he said.

"Yep."

"Barely big enough for one, let alone two."

James thought he could make room if needed, but said nothing, and felt a pang of guilt. He had told Paul that he wouldn't entertain the thought of other guys while they were still together, and here he was on his second full day at university doing just that. But then he hadn't really counted on being woken up by a good-looking guy in a towel either. Didn't that just happen in the movies?

"I was just wondering," Adam said, "if I could borrow some shower gel? It seems I packed everything except that – either that or it fell out of a bag in the car on the way here. The boot of Dad's car is full of crap, we could easily have missed it."

"Sure."

James walked back into his room to find his shower gel.

"I'll get some when I go out to the shop later," Adam continued, "but I've just been for a run and would rather get showered first."

James walked over to him and handed him the bottle.

"Thanks. I'll bring it back when I'm done."

"You're fine. Keep it. I've got an extra couple of bottles."

"Cheers, mate. Sorry for disturbing you."

Adam turned to leave and then said:

"Hey, do you fancy going for a drink tonight? We're the only ones here so far on this floor, I think. I don't know anyone else and there's nothing to do until Monday."

Going for drinks with strangers was not something that James was used to doing. He found talking to people he didn't know difficult and awkward, and he wasn't sure whether he was feeling up to the task, but he didn't turn Adam down.

"That would be good," he found himself saying.

"Nice one. I'll come for you about eight? Is that all right?"

"That would be good. I'll see you then."

"Cool. Thanks again for the shower gel."

James waved awkwardly as Adam padded his way back to his room and then shut the door. He groaned as he looked at the clock and saw it was just 7am. And

Adam had already been out for a run? Was he mad? James realised if he was going to be woken up early then being greeted by a half-naked handsome man at his door helped ease the pain.

James thought he would try and get another hour or two of sleep before getting up. As he pulled off his jeans again and lay back on the bed, he wondered if Adam would be studying film, too. If so, there was a possibility he might find it hard to concentrate during seminars.

.

2

It was Paul's big moving day. At least, he viewed it as the "big move", but in reality he didn't have much to transfer from the bedroom he had shared with James to his small bedsit. But still, moving into his own place seemed like a big thing.

James's mum had ferried Paul's belongings to his new flat by car and had then stayed around long enough to help him unpack some of them, but then she got the feeling that Paul wanted to do the job himself. She had stopped for a coffee and then left him to it.

The sofa and bed he had purchased from a local charity shop had arrived towards the end of the afternoon. The delivery men were not exactly enthusiastic about carrying the furniture up the stairs to Paul's bedsit, claiming issues of "health and safety" and that they wouldn't be covered by insurance if they fell down the stairs. In the end, a five pound note in the hand of each of the delivery men somehow wiped their memories of such issues and Paul's flat found itself "furnished."

He still had the small TV and DVD player that he'd had in his bedroom when he had lived with his parents, and so he had set that up in the lounge area. It really wasn't big enough for a normal-sized television, and so it worked well enough. James's mum had bought him a small dining table and a couple of chairs as a leaving/house-warming present, and the kitchen already came equipped with a cooker, fridge-freezer and washing machine.

By teatime, the move was complete, and everything was unpacked.

It seemed odd.

Paul was now in his own little place, the first time he had a space that he could call his own since his dad had chucked him out a couple of years earlier. However, suddenly he realised that this wasn't what he really wanted. He wanted the flat, yes. But not on his own. This should have been somewhere which he shared with his boyfriend. That was what he really wanted, not a place on his own. Without James he suddenly felt lost. They had been such a part of each other's lives for over two years. He simply wasn't quite sure of what he was meant to do on his own. There was no-one to talk to. No-one to watch movies with.

He was alone.

Paul decided that perhaps the best thing to do to settle himself in was to have something to eat. His first meal. That would make the place seem more homely.

He looked at the clock, and decided that a takeaway was probably his best bet after a long day. He could christen the kitchen later. Just as he was about to leave to walk down the road to the local fish 'n' chip shop, his mobile rang. It was James.

"Hey," Paul said, trying to sound considerably more cheerful than he felt.

"Hi. Are you OK? How did the move go?"

Paul flopped down on the sofa and put his feet up.

"Well, I'm here," he said. "Everything's been delivered that should have been delivered, which is a miracle, and everything's unpacked."

"How does the furniture look? Does it fit in there OK?"

"Yeah, it's good, I think. Won't know properly for a few days. Your mum was great."

"She always is! You managed to do all of that quickly."

"We started early, and it's not like I had much stuff."

"Sorry I didn't call before." James said. "I've been really tired."

"You texted, it's cool. Are you all right?"

"Yeah. It's just all a bit strange really."

"Same here. How's uni? Have you managed to settle in OK?"

Paul heard James stretching on the other end of the phone.

"Getting there, I guess. The beds are absolutely shit, Paul."

"I've got a nice comfy one," came the response.

"That's right, rub it in. I wish I was there to share it with you."

"Me, too. You mean you don't like it there?" Paul tried not to sound as if he was happy that James might not like being away from home.

"I don't know. I've not had time to find out yet. Nothing really gets going until Monday. I hadn't even met anyone else until this morning."

"Who was that?"

"The guy in the room next door. He came to borrow some shower gel."

"That sounds like the start of a dodgy porn movie."

"You should know. You watch enough!" James joked. "I can assure you that I have been faithful. Don't panic."

"I won't." Paul got up off the sofa and slipped into a jacket and headed for the door. "We'll have to talk while I walk to the chippy, or they're going to be shut by the time I get there."

"Sorry. I was going to call later, but the guy next door has asked me to go for a drink with him tonight. I wasn't going to say yes, but for some reason I did, and he'll be here in an hour or so."

Paul hurried down the stairs and into the street and started walking towards the shops.

"Ah. So you *have* got a new man, then?" he said, already picturing a worst case scenario of James canoodling with the mystery man.

"No. I'm just being friendly. Don't be paranoid! Besides, I'm sure you're only going to the chippy because of the new guy they've got working in there."

"Oh, I'd forgotten about him. All six-foot-six of him. Now there's an idea."

"I wouldn't get too excited, he'll smell of fish."

"You always have to spoil things. I'll wear a clothes-peg on my nose. But, anyway, enjoy your first night at the uni bar, and I'll call you tomorrow."

"Will do. Enjoy your night of passion with the fishy man!"

"Don't get too drunk."

"As if! Miss you."

"Miss you too."

And he did, more than James could imagine.

3

Jason Mitchell paid for the drinks and walked across the pub to the table in the corner that Madeline had chosen for them. He put the drinks on the table and then sat down, staring at the pretty girl opposite him, and wondering what he had done to deserve a date with her. Perhaps he had managed to turn things around, after all.

"So…" he said.

"So?"

"Yeah."

Madeline looked at him with surprise, and then couldn't stop herself from laughing.

"Jason Mitchell, are you actually nervous?"

Jason took a sip of his drink. Nervous wasn't even a close description of how he felt. This was his first date in two years, and maybe the first one ever that he had really cared about. He had never cared about Claire. As much as he hated to admit it, she had been little more than a prop. Nothing more than proof that he had a girlfriend just like everyone else. Madeline was different.

"No comment," he said, smiling.

"What on earth have you got to be nervous about? It's not like this is a blind date or something. We've known each other for months now."

"I know, I know. I just don't want to screw things up, that's all."

"We're talking, Jason. Over a drink. This is not going to end with a night of passion. We're not going to have sex. If you're lucky, you might be allowed to kiss me goodnight. *Might*. It's a stress-free evening. Nothing to be nervous about."

"I never used to be like this. It's just…"

"Just what?"

It was just that Jason couldn't get out of his head what had happened with Claire. How he had hurt her. How he had coerced her into have sex with him. It all seemed so long ago, but he couldn't forget it. Sometimes he felt as if he didn't want to. He was a different guy now – he believed he would never do stuff like that again, but thought that remembering what he had done might keep him from going back to the person he had been. In fact, he was sure of it. But he was still worried that he might hurt the girl in front of him, even if it was unintentional. He couldn't bear to do that.

"It's just...I don't know," he flustered. "You and Rick and Mark, you've all been so good to me. I don't want to screw things up, that's all."

"You think us being on a 'date' – and I used that term loosely – might screw things up?"

"No. I think *I* might screw things up. Things have got so much better for me since I met the three of you. You have no idea how things were before. I don't want anything to muck that up."

Madeline sat back in her chair and looked at Jason. Who was this guy in front of her? To say he was confusing was an understatement. She had heard so much about him from others, but he seemed nothing like the stories that she had been told.

"You're a mysterious one," she said. "One minute you're a cheeky, cocky little bastard, and then the next you're like a shy and frightened kid. I don't understand you. But you intrigue me."

"I intrigue you?" Jason said. "Is that good or bad?"

"A bit of each, I guess. But we've known each other for a few months now, and you've made sure that we know nothing about you. You never talk about your past. You never talk about your other friends. And you've never mentioned your parents once."

Jason didn't know what he should say, or how

much he should tell her. What could he say that wouldn't drive Madeline away?

"There are no other friends. Not anymore. You're it. You and Rick and Mark. All my old friends are gone. That's the way I want it. They weren't good for me. They got me into trouble," he lied. "It was time to move on. I don't want things to change between us. They're perfect as they are. No complications."

Madeline put her hand on Jason's.

"You're going to have to do better than that," she said.

"What do you mean?"

"I've told two friends that I'm meeting you tonight, for a date. Well, for a date-like thing. Whatever this is. Both told me not to go anywhere near you, to back off, that you were bad news. That you were a horrible guy. I've known you a while, and I haven't seen that. I've not seen anything remotely resembling that. Why would they think that, Jason? What's your story?"

Jason pulled his hand away and finished his drink and then put the glass back down on the table with more force than he intended to. He stood up.

"Come on," he said. "I'll take you home."

"I don't want to go home, Jase. I didn't say I *believed* them."

"Perhaps you should, but I didn't come here to be interrogated."

Jason walked across the pub and out of the door. Madeline looked after him, not really sure of what she should do.

What did he mean by that? What did her friends mean when they told her he was a nasty piece of work? Perhaps she should trust them – she'd known them much longer. But Jason seemed so vulnerable. She couldn't just let him leave.

She quickly put her jacket on and ran of the pub, looking around for Jason. He was about fifty metres down the road, walking quickly towards his house. She shouted after him, but he just kept on walking. She started to run after him, shouting his name again, but he didn't stop. Finally, she caught up with him, and he turned around to face her. Tears were streaming down his face.

"Jason, what on earth is the matter? Tell me what it is," Madeline said.

"Just leave me alone," Jason sobbed.

"Why? What's going on?"

"Your friends were right. You're better off without me."

"I don't believe you, Jason." Madeline walked towards him. "What are you crying about? Don't be upset."

Jason slumped down on the pavement, his back resting against a fence. Madeline squatted down beside him.

"I've been an idiot," Jason said. "I've done some bad things – some *really* bad things. You have no idea who I used to be. I've tried to make things right, I've tried to sort myself out. But they just won't go away. They follow me around everywhere. I hate what I used to be, but I can't escape it."

Madeline was unsure of what to do. She didn't feel she could leave Jason in the state that he was in, and she felt guilty for being curious about Jason's past and what he had done. Surely what he had done couldn't have been *that* bad?

"But what did you do?" she asked.

Jason was about to tell her everything – the whole story about what he was like at school, and what he had done to James and Paul, and even some of his former friends. He could have told her how he had come to his senses when he had to jump into the river to try and save Paul, and how he had changed.

He wiped his eyes.

"I'm not the same guy as I was then," he said.

"What was it? Drugs? I just assumed that what my friends were talking about were drugs."

Jason turned to look at her.

Drugs. A perfect cover story.

His past was tainted because he had been a drug taker when he was younger. How come he hadn't thought of telling her that before? It sure as hell sounded much better than telling her that he used to beat people up, video it and post it on the web, and it was a way of explaining why Madeline's friends thought he was bad news.

He knew deep down that it was the wrong thing to do. He knew he should be telling her the truth, to get it out in the open. That way it wouldn't come back and bite him on the ass later. But it was too much of a risk.

He might lose her.

During the next few seconds, his mind went into overdrive, quickly concocting a past for himself that had never happened. Sure, he'd sold some drugs to other kids at school, but that was hardly the point. He'd make up a whole story.

"Yeah," he finally said. "I used to have a problem with drugs when I was younger. I'm sorry I didn't tell you before. I'm just so ashamed of it. I don't like talking about it now. Things have changed. I've changed, Madeline. You have to believe me."

Madeline did, and Jason knew it. He could see it in her eyes, and she felt sorry for him. He was safe from his past once again.

For now.

4

James and Adam might have been virtually the only people on their floor that morning but, by the evening, all that had changed.

All day, James had heard from his room the sound of people arriving, of suitcases being wheeled across the floor, and of parents saying elongated and emotional goodbyes to their sons and daughters who were probably wishing they would just go home and let them unpack and get down the pub. James had heard lots of crying from both parents and kids, and was now even more glad that he had come to campus on his own without his mum and Paul in tow. Getting them to leave would have been nigh on impossible. It would have been traumatic for everyone conceived.

James hid in his room for most of the day. He was extra tired, and at one point listened to Spotify with his headphones in to drown out the noise from the corridor and woke up about an hour and a half later. He knew he had been woken up early by Adam, but it wasn't as if he had been to bed late the night before – quite the opposite, in fact. He had been in bed long before midnight, and he was normally something of a night owl.

James put the tiredness down to the uncomfortable bed and the new surroundings, and maybe even nerves played a part in it. Sadly, the sleep during the afternoon hadn't helped either. He began to wish that he had turned down Adam's offer of going for a drink in the evening. He could have done with a quiet night. Getting enough sleep was important, he knew that. But he felt he couldn't tell Adam he had changed his mind. They had only just met, and he didn't want him to think he was unreliable.

When they arrived at the university bar just after eight o'clock, they stood in the doorway in shock. They had expected it to be relatively busy, but they were amazed at how many people could be crammed into one place.

"Wow," James said, staring. "Have they never heard of fire regulations?"

"Do you want to go somewhere else?" Adam asked.

James desperately wanted to say "yes." He hated crowded places at the best of times, and had suffered what he could only assume were panic attacks in such environments before. However, he was determined not to let such things affect him at university. It was his big chance to fight the demons that had been plaguing him for months. This was part of moving on.

"No," he said, taking a deep breath. "Let's do it."

They stepped forward and slowly but surely squeezed (and occasionally pushed and shoved) their way to the bar, and knew that they were in for a long wait as the crowd there was three or four people deep. That wasn't too bad when they were on the outside, but the closer they got to the bar, the more hemmed in James felt. He started to sweat, rolled up his sleeves, and undid the top button on his shirt. Before long, he could feel his heart racing and he was visibly trembling.

Adam glanced over at him.

"Are you OK?" he asked. "I can get these if you want. You could go and find a table or a chair...well, *somewhere* to sit!"

James smiled nervously at him and pulled out his wallet.

"If you don't mind. That would be good."

"It's fine. What do you want?"

"Just a lager. I don't care what it is as long as it's cold."

He pulled out a five-pound note and held it towards Adam.

"Here," he said.

"No. Put it in your wallet, you can get the next round."

James edged his way out of the crowd and looked around for somewhere to sit. He saw a couple of people leaving at the far end of the room and made his way there as quickly as he could and sat down, putting his jacket on the other seat to indicate it was taken.

He closed his eyes to clear his mind as best as he could, and started doing his deep-breathing exercises, hoping that no-one would notice. He wiped the sweat from his face, and slowly started to feel himself calm down. Adam sat down at the table about five minutes later.

"I got here eventually!" he said as he sat down.

"Do you think it's like this every night, or is it just because it's the beginning of semester?"

"No idea. I'm not really a big drinker, if I'm being honest, so it won't make much difference to me."

"I'm not either," James said. "I'd rather have a cup of tea."

"I'm with you on that one. We should try and find a nice café for next time. Anyway, cheers."

The boys clinked their glasses together and then tried to get used to the madness that surrounded them. Some groups of people clearly knew each other well and were excited to see each other after the summer break, whereas others were more like James and Adam, and spending their first few hours together with their flat mates.

"You have a problem with crowds?" Adam asked.

"Yeah," James admitted. "I should have said."

"It's cool. I have a cousin who does, too. He fainted when I was out Christmas shopping with him once. It's no big deal. We all have things that make us nervous."

"Thanks."

"What are you studying?"

"Film and television. And you?"

"American Studies. That probably means we'll be sharing some of the same units this year, right? Don't you have to do a course on 20th Century American history as part of your first semester?"

"I haven't checked yet."

"I think you do. It'll be useful to know at least one person on the course!"

James smiled.

"Yes," he said.

"Did your parents bring you and your stuff here?

"No," James said. "I came on the train on my own. They would have come with me, but I couldn't cope with all the crying from my mum and my other half."

James wondered why he didn't just say "boyfriend."

"I don't blame you. I didn't have that luxury. My mum and dad insisted on bringing me. There were plenty of tears, from my dad mostly. He wasn't keen on me going out into the big wide world. He thinks I am going to get corrupted."

"It's as big a thing for them as it is for us, I guess."

"That's true. But I'm glad to get away, to be honest. There have been quite a few tensions at home lately.

Lots of arguments about…well, church…and me and my brother's decision not to go anymore. That was a year ago, but they still haven't got over it yet. They view it as a two-finger salute to how we were brought up. But it isn't that. University is freedom – a chance to not have religion shoved down our throats. I'm not even out at home. My folks would go nuts if they knew. But here I can do what I want without looking over my shoulder all the while."

"Here's hoping," James said, curious that Adam was telling him this so early in their friendship. Did he already realise that James was gay?

"I guess we're all excited to be leaving home, right?" Adam said.

James realized that most people probably were, but he wasn't sure if he was. Everyone around him in the bar seemed happy to be there, but that wasn't the way that he was feeling. It wasn't even as if he was nervous. He just wondered if he had made the right decision in going to university at all, but, at least for tonight, Adam was providing good company.

CHAPTER FIVE

1

Jonathan opened the bathroom door, still wet from taking a shower, and a towel wrapped tightly around his waist. When he had gone for a shower, his boyfriend had still been in bed with seemingly no intention of getting out of it. Jonathan very much doubted that situation had changed within the last few minutes.

"Are you up yet?" he called through to Andrew as he dried his hair with a towel.

Andrew was not anything like close to getting up. In fact, he had every intention of staying in bed for as much of the day as possible.

"Yes," he called back. "I'm now coming."

Jonathan was well aware that the comment meant that Andrew hadn't moved since he had left the room. He swore to himself quietly, and walked down the hallway to the bedroom.

"I heard that," Andrew said. "If you're going to

swear about me, at least do it to my face."

Jonathan stood in the bedroom doorway and looked at Andrew, his worst fears realised.

"Fine," he said. "Get out of bed you bloody lazy bastard."

Andrew stared at him.

"There was a time when seeing you in just a towel would have produced a reaction," he said. He pulled back the duvet and patted his hand on the boxer shorts he had slept in. "But look. Nothing."

"Perhaps your penis is as unwilling to get up as the rest of you," Jonathan said, sarcastically.

Andrew closed his eyes and rolled over.

"You're meant to be nice to me. I'm ill," he said, and pulled the duvet back over himself tightly.

"Yes. And you're a bloody awful patient. You need to get up. I'm not joking."

"I'm signed off work, remember? I don't *need* to do anything. Just leave me alone. I'll get up when I'm ready."

"You do have to get up, actually. You have an assessment for counselling at ten o'clock, and I have no intention of letting you be late for it."

"Yeah, right. The doctor said it would be months before I was seen. Even you can't do magic tricks like that."

"No, she said it would be months before you had the proper sessions. But they rang first thing and said they had a cancellation for an assessment this morning."

"Yeah, someone probably jumped off a multi-story

car park after waiting so long for a bloody appointment."

Jonathan was beginning to lose his temper. They only had ninety minutes to get Andrew in the shower, dressed, and to the appointment. He was serious when he said he wasn't going to let him be late.

"Come on, it's time for getting out of bed, going into the shower, and getting ready for this appointment. I've taken the morning off work so that I can take you."

This wasn't quite true, he had just rearranged his shift slightly. But that was beside the point.

"I can get there myself. I'm not senile. I don't need a parent to take me."

"I'm going to give you support."

"And to make sure I actually go."

"That, too."

"I'm not stupid."

"You said that before."

Jonathan sighed. Trying to help Andrew was more difficult than he could have imagined. He walked over to the bed and sat down.

"I'm like this because I love you," he said.

Andrew lay still on the bed.

"I know."

Jonathan leant over and kissed him, and then stood up and pulled the duvet on to the floor.

"Time to move," he said. "And time to get you out of these boxers. You've been wearing them all weekend. They stink, Andrew."

He quickly tugged at the boxer shorts and pulled

them off, throwing them across the room.

"Fine," Andrew said. "It looks like I have no choice, doesn't it?"

"Now you're learning."

Jonathan looked down at Andrew who was now naked on the bed.

"It seems like there's life under those boxer shorts, after all," he said

"Is there life under that towel?"

Jonathan let the towel drop to the floor.

"Always," he said. "I'll prove it to you when we get you in the shower."

2

James and Adam had assumed that registering at the university would be an exciting moment – officially signing their name to say they had arrived and eager to see what the next three years might bring.

The reality was rather different.

There were queues across campus as other first year students from all the different departments stood in line to do the same thing. The one for James' and Adam's snaked throughout the ground floor of the building and about fifty metres outside. Word fed back to them through the queue as they stood in the rain that the computer system had "gone down," which had caused the holdup. Neither of them thought that a failing computer system was a good advertisement for an institution to which they were about to pay nine thousand pound a year for tuition. Computers always seemed to pick the worst moments to go wrong, and in this case it was bad for both the university and the students.

James wasn't feeling great to start with. He had barely slept at all the night before. He had gone to bed early again in the hope that he would feel more energetic the next day. However, he was still struggling with the ridiculously small and uncomfortable bed, plus the students on the floor above had decided to throw a party. James wasn't sure what this party might have involved (although he admitted he was curious to find out), but every time he nodded off, someone shouted or screamed and woke him up. And now he realised that he would have to stand in the rain for what could be hours. It was true to say that it wasn't the start to his first full week at university that he had envisaged.

Things could only get better.

Up ahead, a student walked out of the registration building, and the queue shuffled forward a metre or so – at least a small sign that progress was being made, but James decided that he'd had enough.

"Do you think we should come back later?" he said to Adam, hoping he would take the hint. "We could go and have a coffee and then come back? The queue might be shorter then. We're going to get soaked if this rain gets any worse."

James felt he really could do with some caffeine to

keep him awake and give some energy. His legs felt as if they were going to give way.

The line shuffled forward another few inches.

"I don't know," Adam replied. "It looks like we're moving a bit quicker now."

This was the problem of James doing this with someone he had only just met. He simply didn't have the balls to say what he was really feeling – that he was too tired to stand any longer – in case it made him look bad. No, it wasn't that he would look bad, it was that he would be embarrassed by admitting how he was feeling.

He hadn't felt that he could say no to registering with Adam either. It would have been different if it had been Paul standing beside him.

James didn't want to push away the only friend that he had at university. He was sure he would make more but, by living in adjoining rooms, they had been thrown together and it had prevented the effort of trying to mix with other people – something James had trouble doing. That didn't stop James wishing he was doing this on his own, though.

He was beginning to realise that travelling a couple of hours away from home hadn't resulted in him leaving behind the problems that had plagued him for the last year or so.

The tiredness.

The lack of energy.

The nightmares.

The panic.

The suitcase of belongings that he had brought with

him hadn't been big, but it appeared that he had brought some other baggage too, if only in his mind. He had expected a new start, and he was still hoping for one, but he realised now, after just a few days, that things were not going to be quite that easy.

Ironically, despite everything he wanted to leave behind, he was already missing home. Especially his mum and Paul. And he felt lost without the safety net that the counselling he had been having had provided. Each week, no matter how difficult things had been, he had known that he could talk away some of his troubles on a Tuesday afternoon. Now that had gone, and if felt like it had left a giant hole.

There were times when he almost grudged the fact that Paul seemed to be coping with everything so well. Despite all that had happened to Paul at school, and at home with his parents, he seemed to have no long-lasting effects of it. *He* didn't have the nightmares, or a distrust of everyone and everything around him. Just James. And he was *so* tired of it. Fighting those feelings and trying to cope with the endless anxiety day after day just seemed to sap him of energy and enthusiasm for everything - including standing in a queue for hours.

"I'm sorry," he said to Adam, finally. "I'm not feeling too good. I didn't get much sleep last night. With that party upstairs."

"Yeah," Adam replied. "Someone in the kitchen said they were making a row. Mum had the sense to pack me a few packets of ear plugs. Apparently, she remembered how noisy it could get in campus accommodation. I used them last night. Slept like a baby."

James wondered why he hadn't thought of something so simple. Rachel, his sister, could have recommended them, having been in university halls already.

"I never thought of that," he said. "I'll have to get some."

"You can have a pack of mine. Mum packed loads. It will pay you back for the shower gel."

James smiled.

"Cheers. That would be great."

Adam put his hand on James's shoulder.

"You look like crap, to be honest," he said.

"Thanks. You know how to cheer someone up."

"We can go and get a drink and a sit down before we do this if you want. I really don't mind. You should have said you weren't feeling up to much."

James nearly cried with relief.

"That would be great," he said.

They stepped out of the queue, much to the pleasure of those standing behind them who took a few steps forward, and made their way to the main square of the university where there were several places they could get a drink or something to eat. The first two they went to were busy, but finally they went to the main restaurant, which was now in between serving breakfast and lunch (and didn't have the same array of coffees as the other cafes), and so was relatively deserted.

James and Adam got a table in a corner, away from

other people, where they could talk without shouting.

"I'm sorry about that," James said.

"It doesn't bother me," Adam replied. "But you should have said you weren't feeling well."

James wanted to explain everything – that he hadn't felt ill, as such, but that he had panic attacks and got tired easily, and didn't really know why. The doctor had called it depression – but the doctor hadn't known much about what James had gone through in school and how he couldn't forget about it.

He would have loved to have told Adam about it. He felt that he would understand, somehow, but the truth was that he couldn't be bothered. Everything was too much effort, even talking felt like hard work. And once he started talking about that stuff, then he had to mention other things, too, like Jason. And Paul. He hadn't mentioned to Adam that he had a boyfriend, and he wasn't sure why. Perhaps it was because dropping Paul's name into the conversation might make it look like he thought Adam was coming on to him. Or perhaps that was just part of the life back at home that he was trying to forget about. But he felt guilty for thinking that. Besides, he didn't want to come across to Adam like a sob story on a talent show.

"Are you missing home?" Adam asked him.

"Honestly? No. I don't think so. I'm missing my bed, though! I'd give anything for a comfy bed."

"I'm with you on that."

"It's just weird being here. A new place, not really knowing anyone, except yourself, of course."

"Yeah, the only guy you know is the one who knocks on your door nearly naked at the crack of dawn to borrow some shower gel. I'm sorry about that, by the way. I was such an idiot; I just didn't think that other people might still be asleep. We're always up at the crack of dawn at home."

"Don't worry about it. It's fine."

"Which bit? Waking you up or being nearly naked?" Adam smiled as he asked the question. "At least it worked by means of an introduction."

"Cheeky," James replied, unwilling to answer the question.

"The Soc Mart is this afternoon," Adam said. "If you want to go? I wanted to join the Pride Society, but honestly don't want to do it on my own. It's a big thing for me. Would you come with me? I don't want to impose, though. You don't have to."

"Pride Society? Is that what they call it now?"

"I think the LGBT acronym got too long, so they've gone with an easier option. Will you come with me?" he asked again. "It's fine if you think you'll be tired or worn out or whatever. But thought I'd ask."

Despite the fact that James would have liked nothing more than to stay in bed all afternoon and catch up on some sleep, he agreed to go with Adam. Firstly, he was determined not to let his tiredness and panic get the better of him, and, secondly, he already knew just how much being able to join a group like the Pride Society would mean to Adam, given how he wasn't able to be out at home.

It had been over two years since James had come out, and sometimes he still wondered how he had managed to hide things from his mum and sister for so long, and, unlike Adam, he had always known deep down that there was almost no chance that his mum would have had a problem with him being gay. He remembered what had happened to Paul when his dad found out about his sexuality. He had been chucked out of his own home.

"It's OK," he said. "I'll come with you. We'll go and register after we finish here, then I'll go back to my room and have a sleep for a couple of hours, and then we can head to Soc Mart later in the afternoon. Is that OK?"

Adam smiled.

"Perfect," he said.

3

"What are you drawing?"

It was Mark who asked the question. Jason was eating lunch at college with him, Rick and Madeline. Or, rather, they were eating lunch while Jason drew in his notepad. He spent most of his free time that way. It made him relax, and after the date with Madeline, he *needed* to relax.

"None of your business," Jason said to him, a little bit more curtly than he had planned to.

"Alright, keep your hair on."

"Sorry, I didn't mean it to come out like that."

"Is that what you said to Madeline on your date?"

Jason glared at him. He knew that Mark was only joking, but he didn't approve of joking in that way where Madeline was concerned. She was out of bounds when it came to that kind of joke.

Madeline put her hand on Jason's knee and squeezed it.

"I understand why you are trying to find out that kind of information, Mark," she said

"Oh, yeah? Why is that?"

"Because hearing about Jason's date with me is the nearest you're going to get to having one of your own. Helps with your little fantasies." She leaned towards Mark. "Helps get the blood pumping," she said in a whisper.

Jason couldn't help but smile.

Madeline was everything that Claire, his previous girlfriend, hadn't been. Independent. Ballsy. Quick-witted. A tease. She reminded him of Jane, not that he had seen her or Luke for a long time. And he hadn't seen Claire for even longer. But thoughts of Claire had kept bugging him for the last few days, since he had lied to Madeline about his past. He regretted that lie now. This was meant to be a fresh start, and he dreaded making the same mistakes with Madeline that he had with Claire. No matter what he had thought of her, he should never have treated her the way he had.

He still couldn't get the night that he and Claire had

sex out of his head. What the hell had he been thinking? He wondered if he should try to contact her again, to try to explain things. To try to say sorry again. But how would that look to Madeline if she found out? She would hardly want him making contact with his ex-girlfriend just as they were starting to go out.

The night with Claire had also been the last time Jason had had sex. And the first time. While he liked Madeline a lot, he was worried about what would happen if and when they came to have sex for the first time. He was worried that he might not be able to get the time with Claire out of his head – a time when he couldn't perform and so he took out his frustrations on her. He had screwed things up again, and there was an inevitability that his latest lie would be his undoing.

"Are you OK for Friday, Jason?" Rick asked.

Jason didn't answer.

"Earth calling Jason."

He waved his hands in front of Jason's face.

"Are you alright?" he said.

"Yeah, yeah. Just miles away."

"He was thinking about Madeline," Mark said.

"Will you just shut up?" Jason snapped at him.

"What the hell has got into you today?"

"Nothing. You just never stop sometimes. You can be so juvenile."

Jason hated himself for saying it as soon as the words had left his mouth.

"Juvenile," Mark said. "Long word for you."

"Friday. Poker," Rick said. "Are you up for it?"

"Yeah, yeah, of course. Looking forward to it. Sorry, just got other things on my mind, that's all."

"Why don't you sit for me this afternoon?" Madeline said to him. "Your mind can drift all it wants as long as you sit still."

"Yeah, that sounds good actually."

On any other day, Mark would have made a sarcastic, innuendo-laden remark about Jason modelling for Madeline, but he knew from how Jason had snapped at him that it was probably best that he kept his humour for another day.

4

After a much-needed sleep, James met Adam at the Soc Mart, as arranged, late that afternoon. Adam had got there a bit earlier and had been on a wander around, and now he took James on a whistle-stop tour of the event.

At first, James thought the event was going to be something of a chore, but soon he got more interested and couldn't believe just how many societies were on offer, ranging from the obvious to the downright bizarre.

There were those for sports, some of which neither he nor Adam had heard of. Adam spent a few minutes talking to those at the table for the Running Society, who told him about the various activities they organized, including park runs and early morning jogs for those that were interested in those. Adam signed up, although James jokingly reminded him that he didn't want to be woken up every morning so that Adam could borrow some shower gel after he had been on a run.

There were a number of groups that fell somewhat loosely under the banner of faith and religion, and in each case both James and Adam walked straight past. James wouldn't have been interested anyway, but Adam was adamant given his home life that the last thing he wanted to be involved with at university was religion.

James *was* interested in some of the political groups, though. He had begun getting more interested in politics over the last couple of years, and had taken the subject at A-level. He put his name down for the rather wide-ranging Politics Society, and found himself chatting to a member of the Better Politics Society.

"What does the Society do?" he asked.

"We're not quite sure," came the reply. "This is the first year it's been run. So, it's a bit of a work in progress. We went down to London for some protests, and thought we should turn it into a soc."

"Have you had many sign up?"

"Not a huge amount, yet. But it's still early days. We've got more people than them, though."

The girl gestured towards the Jacob Rees-Mogg Society.

James smiled.

"Not many of his fans at uni?"

"I don't think they're overrun with queries."

"What were the protests like?" James asked.

"Awesome. And great fun. And so many people."

"Wish I had been there."

"You want to sign up in case we go again?"

James said that he did, and wrote down his name and email address.

"If ever I end up going to London to protest against anything, I'm not going to tell my mum," he said to Adam. "She'd freak out in case I got arrested or something!"

"You should be so lucky. Nice policemen in uniform. Perhaps there'll be something you can protest about locally instead."

The event had something of a carnival atmosphere. There was one of the university's jazz bands playing at the far end of the room, and everyone around James seemed happy and excited to be there, including Adam. James was finding it interesting, but was struggling again with the sheer amount of people there. The Circus Society table was manned by two students on stilts, and the RAG Society had a young guy locked in some stocks, with the invite to pay one pound to throw a wet sponge at him, or two pounds to plant a custard pie in his face. All proceeds were being donated to a local homeless charity.

"That looks fun," Adam said as they walked past.

"Throwing things at him or being in the stocks?" James asked.

"Both, probably," Adam replied.

"Really?"

James wasn't sure if Adam was being serious or not.

"Oh, I'm full of surprises!" Adam said, and winked at James.

"Kinky," James replied, not sure whether to take the comment seriously or not.

They both joined the Film Society, and then finally made their way to the Pride Society, which was at the far end of the room. As they signed up, they were given a flyer telling them of an icebreaker social taking place that weekend.

"Can we go together to the icebreaker?" Adam asked James as they walked out of the building and started on the way back to their rooms. "Will you come with me? I'll be nervous going on my own."

James felt he couldn't refuse.

"OK," he said. "But you need to know I have a boyfriend."

Adam didn't seem surprised.

"I guessed that much. I'd have been surprised if someone hadn't snapped you up already," he said. "How long have you been together?"

"A couple of years. He's been living at our house for most of that time."

"You had a live-in boyfriend at sixteen?" Adam asked with amazement.

James laughed.

"It's not quite what it sounds like. It's all rather a long and complicated story. I'll tell you about it at some point."

"Intriguing," Adam said, as they got back to their rooms. "I'll see you tomorrow?"

"Sure. We both have to be at the introductory lecture anyway."

James went back into his room and sat down on the bed. He woke up seven hours later at 2am, and headed to the kitchen to get something to eat to tide him over until the morning.

5

Jonathan had stayed at work later than he had planned to, and yet still was not keen on going home.

After Andrew's appointment with the counselling service that morning, he had wondered again if he had bit off more than he could chew in saying that he wanted to help his boyfriend through his problems.

He and Andrew had now been together for nearly two and a half years, and it hadn't been an easy relationship for either of them – something not helped by it being Andrew's first so late in life. That had created all kinds of issues – some expected, some less obvious - that both of them had worked through together. The same was true of the problems at the school that had ultimately helped to bring them together in the first place. But what was happening now was different.

Both he and Andrew knew that the meeting with the counselling service wouldn't lead to anything regular with them straight away, but being told that again by the counsellor during the session had made

Andrew come out in a worse state than he had gone in. He had seemed somewhat surprised that the wait would be a year or more, even though he had already been told that by his GP. Perhaps he had thought that she had only told him that so he didn't get expectations raised.

Jonathan hadn't gone in with him, but had sat patiently in the waiting room, constantly wondering what Andrew might have been telling the counsellor and whether it was the truth or not. The stage had been reached where Jonathan didn't care what the truth was as long as Andrew was being completely honest about it.

When they had got home, Jonathan had gone online and looked at the options for private counselling. Andrew was less than keen on this, despite the fact that Jonathan made the point that they both had a good income and could easily afford it, even if only for a relatively limited time, but Jonathan wasn't sure whether it was in fact the financial issue that was making Andrew wary. He also wasn't sure whether Andrew would have been any happier if the counselling service had told him earlier in the day that they had a slot for him starting the following week.

Jonathan had hoped that the initial session would have got Andrew more enthusiastic, but that seemingly hadn't happened. It was becoming very clear that he just wanted to lie around the house all day. Jonathan realised that fatigue and a lack of energy came with the health problem itself, but he was also frustrated that Andrew seemed unwilling to try and help himself – and all of this despite the rather frank talk they'd had just a few days earlier.

Jonathan knew from his chat with the headteacher at the school that Andrew had been lying to him, or, to be more charitable, not been telling him the whole truth. Getting through Andrew's health problems was going to be far easier if he was honest about what was going on and how he felt.

These thoughts had been playing on Jonathan's mind all day at work, and, as he sat in the car on the way home, he secretly hoped he would catch every red light, and that there might be roadworks that slowed the traffic down. He had promised Andrew he would stand by him, but somehow, he also had to get the message across that he would only do so if he was honest with him – and he had no idea how to do that without causing yet another row.

Perhaps he would leave that conversation for another day, after all.

CHAPTER SIX

1

Adam was awoken at half past three in the morning by the sound of screaming. It wasn't the screaming of a group of fellow students who were a little bit tipsy and having a good time elsewhere in the building. This was someone screaming in absolute fear.

Adam was instantly awake, and he pulled back the duvet and got out of bed, pulling on some boxer shorts before opening the door to his room and going out into the hallway. He realised he must have been sleeping soundly, as there were already several people in the corridor who were trying to work out what all the noise was about and what they should do. Presumably, the noise had been carrying on for some time.

The screams were coming from James's room, and Adam went up to his door and started knocking on it, worried that his new friend was being attacked.

"James! Are you OK?"

The screams had turned to little more than a whimper by this point, but there was no reply from James. Still worried, Adam tried again, this time banging hard on the door.

"JAMES!"

The noises stopped, and Adam began to realise that the likelihood was that James had been simply having a nightmare. Or, at least, he hoped that was the case.

"James? Are you alright?" he asked, quieter this time.

He heard movement within the room, and gestured for the other students in the corridor to go back inside.

"He's OK. Just a bad dream, I think," Adam told them.

Eventually, James opened his door. He had pulled on some jeans, but was shirtless, and his chest was soaked in sweat. His hair was matted to his head, and Adam could see into the room enough to notice that the sheet covering the mattress was also soaked in sweat, and that the duvet was on the floor.

"Hey," James said, rather sheepishly.

"Hey," Adam replied. "Are you alright?"

"Yeah, sorry. Just a bad dream. Sorry I woke you, Adam."

"I woke *you* once, remember? Do you need anything? Is there anything I can do? I can sit with you for a bit if you want. I don't mind."

The fact that James knew that Adam was being totally genuine in his offer made it even worse for him. James would have liked to have asked him in and to have some company for a little while, but the only thing he could think of was Paul back at home. James couldn't allow himself to get any closer to Adam, even if it might have been the right thing to do at that moment.

"Thanks," James said. "But I'll be OK. I have nightmares quite often. I'll have a shower to freshen up and then try to get some sleep. I'll see you in the morning?"

Adam nodded.

"Yeah. The coffee shop at noon, like we arranged."

"I'll see you there."

James closed the door, and Adam turned to the others that were still standing in the hallway.

"Back to bed, folks. The show's over," he said as he went back to his own room.

2

"Are you feeling better?" Adam asked James as he sat down across the table from him at the coffee shop later that morning.

James smiled.

"Yeah, thanks. I'm really sorry about that. I didn't intend to wake up half the floor."

"I don't think they have much room to complain given how noisy some of them have been. The main thing is that you're alright. I think a couple of people were worried you were being murdered."

"Perhaps I was in my dream! Who knows!"

"You don't remember?"

James shook his head.

"No," he lied. "Not really. Most people don't remember their dreams, do they?"

"I have the occasional good one that my brain tries to remember," Adam said with a grin. "And I'm sure I'm not the only one."

James took a sip of his coffee.

"Oh, I can't think about that sort of thing this early in the day!" he said.

The problem was that James *could* remember his dream. He had dreamed that the footage that Jason had shot in the changing rooms at school two years earlier had found its way on to Adam's phone and he had started showing it to people at the university. There were so many times when his dreams seemed to be telling him not to trust people, and he had always assumed this was due to when Paul had betrayed him.

James's mobile phone started vibrating in his pocket and he pulled it out to see who it was.

"Do you need to take that?" Adam asked.

James saw that the caller was Paul, refused the call, and put the phone back in his pocket.

"No, it's just my boyfriend."

"*Just* your boyfriend? That's not very nice!"

"What I meant was that it's not important. I can ring him back later."

"Not important? You're digging yourself a hole about your boyfriend, you know?"

"Oh, shhh."

They sat there quietly for a minute or two, drinking their coffees and watching people go past the window. Campus seemed to be slowly settling into a routine, now. The excited hustle and bustle of the first couple of days had died down. The freshers were now starting lectures, with seminars starting the following week, and the rest of the students had spent the weekend seeing the friends that they hadn't seen all summer and were now ready for university to begin properly once again.

"Are you missing him?" Adam asked, eventually.

"Paul? Yes, of course. To be honest, I miss everything about home, right now. I'm not finding it easy here – but life wasn't very easy back home either. One way or another, I've got to work through it. And I haven't even been here a week yet, so it's early days, I guess. I'm sure it's just a matter of time."

"A long-distance relationship can't be easy."

"That's what Paul keeps telling me – that we won't be able to make it work. But we want to give it a shot. If it's not working out for one of us, I guess we'll try and sort it out. Cross that bridge when we come to it. And what about you? Are you hoping to find the man of your dreams while you're here?"

"I'm not sure how to even start. Never even been close to chatting guys up before."

"Well, perhaps they'll chat you up instead. There was that girl in the registration queue yesterday who took rather a liking to you, I think. So perhaps a guy will too!"

Adam laughed, and nearly spilt his coffee.

"I thought I was just imagining it. Didn't realise you'd noticed it, too."

"You obviously charmed her. Just think, if only it was her you lived next to instead of me, she'd have woken up to you half naked and knocking on her door asking for shower gel on her first day!"

"You're not going to let me forget that, are you?"

"Nope."

"Well, I only had boxers on when I banged on your door last night."

"I'm afraid I don't think I even noticed. You could have got dressed first."

"I thought you were being murdered."

"I don't think you in your boxers is likely to frighten a murderer off."

"Might have distracted him, though, right?"

The problem was that it was *James* who was getting distracted by Adam and he felt guilty about it.

"I wouldn't like to say," he said. "But people might start talking if you keep wandering around with no clothes on."

"I was hoping it might encourage the others on the floor to start doing the same."

"You should be so lucky," James said.

Adam forced a smile.

"To be honest, last night was a nightmare for both of us," he said.

"What do you mean?"

Adam wasn't sure if he should carry on, but felt he

needed to tell someone what had happened.

"I joined Grindr."

"Oh, did you? Is it as full of weird creeps as people say?"

"I don't know. Hard to tell, I guess. But the first message I got was a photo of a man standing naked with a pair of handcuffs in his hands."

James grimaced.

"That's an interesting start to a conversation."

"His profile said he was 39. But he looked as if he was in his fifties."

"Gross. Anyone else?" James asked, realising by the look on Adam's face that there was more to the story than he was telling.

"I was an idiot."

"What do you mean?"

"I got talking to this other guy. He said he was at the uni. He seemed really nice. He sent a picture."

"Of what?"

"His face! He asked me if I wanted to meet him, and I said yes. It was so stupid. I got carried away, I guess. I wouldn't have done it under normal circumstances."

"What happened?"

"We arranged to meet by the coffee shop on campus. I walked there, and I could see him standing there from a distance, but I just bottled it. I ran back to my room and deleted the app. I feel such a dick for standing him up."

James finished his drink.

"I don't know anything about Grindr, but I'm sure you're not the only guy to not turn up to a meeting."

"I've never done anything with a guy before, though. Or a girl. What was I thinking when I agreed to meet him in the first place? I must have gone nuts!"

"I don't know. We all do things we regret in the spur of the moment. I'm sure this guy will survive the heartbreak of you not turning up."

"I guess," Adam said.

"You'll have plenty of time to meet someone while you're here."

Adam forced a smile.

"I suppose so. But it's alright for you with your live-in lover!"

"You need to hold out for the icebreaker at the weekend. Perhaps you'll meet your own knight in shining armour, there. And you won't be able to do anything stupid because I'll be there!"

"Why do you think I asked you?" Adam said, grinning.

But when Adam went to the icebreaker a few days later, James wasn't with him.

3

Andrew wasn't hungry. He had said this as soon as Jonathan had mentioned that he was going to make him his favourite meal for dinner, but his words had not been heard.

"The smell of what I'm about to cook would make anyone hungry," Jonathan had said.

Andrew had made it clear that he hadn't had an appetite for days, although he knew that Jonathan was already aware of this. Perhaps Jonathan was just stuck at home and bored on his day off, and so cooking dinner was giving him something to do, but he was also trying too hard. His constantly-cheerful demeanor throughout the day didn't fool Andrew – he knew when his boyfriend was irritable and fed up, and, in all likelihood, at his wit's end as to what to do to make Andrew feel better. However, Andrew wasn't just *saying* that he didn't want to eat, and neither was he just not bothering to eat, he really did feel groggy, probably due to the medication, and the last thing he wanted to look at was a plate of food that he felt he had no choice but to eat. If there was one thing he didn't need, it was pressure.

At about half past five, Jonathan shouted through from the kitchen that dinner was nearly ready, and Andrew reluctantly got up and went over to sit at the dining table. They didn't use it often, but Jonathan had insisted today, if only to get Andrew out of the armchair he had been lounging in all day while watching re-runs of decades-old quiz shows.

Jonathan brought the plates of food through and put them down on the table, the one with the smaller portion being placed in front of Andrew. Jonathan sat down opposite him.

"Looks good, doesn't it?" he said, still trying to

sound happy and enthused. "Smells good, too."

Andrew forced a smile.

"Yeah, it looks great," he said, whilst having no idea how he was going to get through the next half an hour.

He reached over and picked up the salt shaker, secretly hoping the lid would fall off and dump the contents onto his dinner, thus making it inedible. It didn't happen.

Jonathan started eating while Andrew poked at the food in front of him with his fork. He noticed that Jonathan was watching him, so he smiled again, and speared a piece of meat with the fork and put it into his mouth. The taste was fine, but as he started chewing, his mouth seemed to get drier each time his teeth came into contact with the meat. He knew it was nothing to do with Jonathan's cooking – in fact, Jonathan managed to cook meat more tender than anyone he had ever known, including his own mother. He drank a mouthful of water in the hope it would help things, and managed to swallow the piece of food with the water. One forkful down, only a couple of dozen more to go. Just to make things worse, Jonathan seemed to be really enjoying the meal he had just spent an hour cooking.

"Hmm… This really is good, isn't it?" he said.

Andrew forced another smile.

"Yeah. It's really nice. But you shouldn't have gone to all this trouble."

"You needed to eat. Having those tablets on a permanently empty stomach isn't doing you any good. It says on the box that you should always take them with food, and I don't think it means a biscuit. No wonder why you feel ill. I knew this would get your appetite back."

Andrew could see no way out but to eat what was put in front of him. Or at least try to. Perhaps the way forward was to have bigger mouthfuls. It might seem like less to wade through if it started disappearing quicker. He forced some meat, potato and vegetables onto his fork and shoved it into his mouth. At first, he thought that a mix of different foods all at once might help things, but the more he chewed, the more he was thinking about the amount still left on his plate.

He felt beads of sweat start to form on his forehead, and by the time he had swallowed what was in his mouth, his shirt was becoming soaked with sweat under his arms and down the centre of his back. Panic was beginning to set it, and Andrew wasn't sure how to stop it.

The third mouthful proved to be one too many. He spit it out back on to the plate in front of him and got up from his chair.

"I can't do this," he said, and walked out of the room.

Jonathan put down his knife and fork and walked after him.

"What do you mean, you can't do this?"

Andrew turned to face him.

"What do you think I mean? I can't eat it. Look at me. I'm soaked with sweat."

"I'll open the windows."

"I'm not hot, you moron, I'm panicking."

Jonathan stared at him, clearly not understanding what he was being told.

"What have you got to panic about? It's only food. I've just spent the last hour cooking that!"

"That's your problem. I told you I wasn't fucking hungry. I wasn't making it up."

He ran up the stairs with more energy than he thought he actually possessed, and Jonathan followed him. Andrew went into the bathroom, opened the medicine cabinet and pulled out the packet of antidepressants.

"What the hell are you doing?" Jonathan said, standing at the bathroom door.

"Shoving these bloody things down the loo."

"Like hell you are."

Jonathan came into the room and grabbed hold of Andrew's arm, knocking the pills onto the floor. He was thankful that they were in blister strips and therefore not wasted. He wasn't so thankful for the slap across the face that came next.

"What the hell was that for?"

"For not bloody listening. You're trying to make me feel guilty for not eating the meal you cooked when you *already knew I didn't want it*. And stop pretending to be so happy when you're at home. It's not going to make *me* any happier. And acting was never your strong point anyway – even when you were in the play at school."

"It was your play! You gave me the part!"

Andrew pushed past him and went to the bedroom and then turned to face him.

"Only because nobody else wanted it!" he shouted, and then went into the room and slammed the door shut behind him.

Jonathan tried to open the door, but realized that Andrew had locked it. He'd been meaning to take the lock off the bedroom door ever since they moved in. Now he wished he had.

He took a deep breath, and tried to calm down. The argument had been stupid, and could have been prevented. He knew that.

"Come on, Andrew," Jonathan said. "Let me in."

"Just leave me alone," came the reply.

"You're going to have to come out some time."

"Not until you've gone to work."

"You'll need to pee."

"I'll open the window and water the garden!"

Jonathan didn't doubt that.

He had no idea how to cope with what was going on. This wasn't what he had bargained for, and he wasn't willing to give in to temper tantrums.

"If you'd have gone to the doctor's earlier, we could have avoided this. If you'd have told me what was going on, we wouldn't be in this mess. I can't believe you kept it to yourself, you selfish bastard. I had to find out you were drinking again from your headteacher."

"Leave me alone!" Andrew shouted back at him from behind the closed door.

"Right," Jonathan said, finally. "Have it your way."

Then he went downstairs, sat down at the table, and finished the rest of his now-cold meal. He didn't know how to deal with what was going on, and he was beginning to wonder if he even wanted to.

4

"And so on to a little bit of information regarding the first screening, which is next Monday. You're going to see a couple of short films to start with, both of which show early marriages of image and sound, and then we have *The Jazz Singer*, generally billed as the first talking film but, as you will see, much of it is, in fact, silent, and as we already know attempts at sound film had been made as early as the 1890s. That's all for now. The reading packs are ready to be picked up in the office, and the first two articles need to be read by the time of your seminar next week. Please see me if there are any queries."

The students in the lecture theatre had started putting their coats on before the lecturer had finished speaking, and James watched as a couple of them walked down to the front of the room to ask a question. The lecture had been an introductory one, lasting less than half an hour, and setting the scene for one of the units that would start in earnest the following week. It had been the first lecture theatre that James had gone in, and he was surprised at the size of it.

James went outside and texted Paul while he walked back to his room, saying that he was sorry for missing his call earlier, and arranging to speak to him via Skype at 7pm.

He had felt guilty for refusing Paul's call, especially as he had no real reason for doing so. Sure, Adam had been with him at the time, but he knew he could have left him for a few minutes in order to take the call. Adam wouldn't have minded. Perhaps the nightmare, which, despite what he had told Adam, he could remember all too clearly, reminded him of home in a way that he didn't want to be. And the thought of speaking to Paul added to that. Oddly, almost inexplicably, Paul seemed like an added pressure that he didn't really need. James was worried about *he* was coping, too.

He had his laptop booted and ready long before the appointed time and started the call a couple of minutes early. Paul answered almost immediately, making James think that he had been sitting by his own computer and eagerly awaiting the chance to speak to him. He wasn't wrong. It made James feel even worse that he hadn't taken the telephone call.

As for Paul, he had felt lost now that he was in his own flat and James wasn't around. Part of him wished that he had stayed living with James's mum. At least it would have given him some company, and they could have missed James together. It was too late now. The contract had been signed. He was stuck there for the time being. How long was the contract for? Three months or six? He couldn't remember. Either way, at the moment it seemed like forever.

Paul waved at James the moment that his face appeared on the screen. It was the first time they had seen each other since James had left for university.

"Hey," Paul said.

James waved back rather awkwardly

"How are you doing?" he asked.

"Good, thanks. And you?"

"Yeah, not too bad," James said. "How's your new flat?"

"It's fine."

"You going to show me around?"

"There's not much to see, to be honest. This is the living area. The sofa turns into a bed." Paul moved the camera around the room so that James could see. Then he got up and moved into the kitchen. "And this is the kitchen," he said. "It's ridiculously small, but it has to do. But it's not like I cook much, is it? And, finally, we have the bathroom."

Paul went to the doorway of the bathroom and pointed the webcam inside.

"Just a shower?" James said. "No bath?"

"No bath," Paul verified. "It sucks, right?"

James nodded in agreement.

"You'll miss that. You'll have to go to Mum's if you want a soak in the tub. She wouldn't mind. No bath here, either," he said. "Just the tiniest shower you could possibly imagine."

"Let me see your room, then."

James gave him a quick look around the room, and

the cupboard-sized bathroom.

"And this bed," he said, sitting down on it, "is the most uncomfortable thing that I have ever tried to sleep on."

"It looks it."

"Small, too."

"No room for me, then, if I came to stay?"

"We'd make room."

"How have your first days at uni been? I bet you've been really busy?"

"Yeah. There's always something going on. We actually started lectures today, though, so hopefully I can try and get into a bit more of a routine now."

"That will suit you better," Paul confirmed, demonstrating just how well he knew his boyfriend.

The comment suddenly made James realise how much he was missing Paul. Not as a boyfriend necessarily, but because he knew the right things to say, and knew how James ticked, and how certain things were difficult for him. That was something he was missing more than anything in the few days he had been away – that safety net of people who were looking out for him.

"Have you made any friends while you've been there?" Paul asked.

James wasn't sure how to answer, and he thought that Paul had noticed the hesitation. He didn't want Paul to assume something had happened between him and Adam.

"There's this guy called Adam who lives next door

who is really nice."

"The boy next door, eh?" Paul was joking on the outside, but was struggling to hide his anxiety about James getting together with someone at university. "Do you like him?" he asked.

"He's just a friend, Paul. If that. I've only just met him. I'm not going to jump into bed with him."

"Of course you're not," Paul said, forcing a smile. "But perhaps you should."

"Yeah, right."

"Hey, I've got the guy from the fish 'n' chip shop to keep me occupied, remember?"

"Ah, yeah. Mr. Fishbreath. You should go for it."

"I'd get free chips."

"Maybe a free sausage. What more could you ask for? You'd even get a night of unbroken sleep without me screaming the house down during a nightmare."

Paul looked concerned.

"Are you still having them?"

"Yeah. As if they were ever going to stop overnight. Apparently, I nearly screamed the place down last night. Adam thought I was being murdered. He'd have banged the door down if he had knocked any harder. Others were woken too."

"Were they ok with it?"

"I think so. They don't have much choice really. Adam offered to sit with me for a bit, but I didn't need that. Besides, I didn't want him coming in here and seeing what state I was really in."

"That was sweet of him anyway."

"Yeah," James said. "It was."

Paul was concerned about James. He knew that the nightmares had been slowly getting worse over the previous few weeks – he'd been woken enough by James having them. He thought that going to university might have been good for him, but that clearly wasn't the case if he was still having them. Or perhaps it was too early to expect a change.

"You should see a doctor," he said to James. "Perhaps they can get you to see a counsellor there like you did here."

"The uni has its own counselling service. I don't think I need a doctor to refer me. But has all of that done me any good? After six months of talking, I'm still panicky, and I'm still anxious. I'm still having nightmares. And that's after all of those sessions."

"Well, counselling hasn't done you any harm, has it?"

James shook his head.

"Not that I know of."

Paul wasn't surprised by what James had told him. He knew him too well. The fact that he hadn't been calling him, or even texting him, every day since he had gone away caused Paul to fear that things weren't going well for his boyfriend. Part of him just wanted to tell James to come home, to leave university for another year. But he also realized that would be the selfish thing to do. James needed to give it as much of a chance as he possibly could, and Paul needed to do everything in his power to help.

"How's Mum?" James asked. "Have you seen her?"

"I saw her earlier today. I popped in for a cup of tea. She's OK. But you need to start worrying about yourself rather than her. She'll be fine."

"And what about you? Will you be fine?"

"I'm always fine," Paul said. "You need to relax."

"Fat chance of that. I'm worried about leaving you and Mum behind. And worried that you'll be wondering what I'm up to here."

"You don't need to worry about that," Paul said, taking a deep breath before talking to James about what he had been thinking about ever since he had left.

They could pretend that things hadn't changed and weren't going to change, but the truth was that they had gone from sleeping in the same bed to sleeping in ones many miles apart. They needed time to adapt. Paul thought he had the answer.

CHAPTER SEVEN

1

James didn't sleep well that night, and it had nothing to do with nightmares on this occasion. Instead, it was the Skype call with Paul that was preying on his mind, along with the fact that he was, basically, single for the first time in over two years.

He had managed to get a couple of hours of sleep just as the sun was rising, but was woken up by the sound of Adam going out for his run. It wasn't that Adam had made much of a noise, but James was sleeping so lightly that the sound of the door to Adam's room opening and closing was enough to wake him. James knew that his neighbour would only be gone for around half an hour, and so decided to get up and have a shower, and then have a cup of tea with Adam when he got back. He could always try and get some sleep later in the day.

He was showered and dressed by the time he heard

Adam return, and so opened the door to his room while Adam was unlocking his own.

"Hi," James said, poking his head out of the door. "Good run?"

"Hey," Adam replied, clearly surprised to see him. "Yeah, it was good thanks. You're up early this morning. Nine o' clock lecture?"

"No. Just couldn't sleep. I'm going to put the kettle on. Do you fancy a cup of tea?"

"That would be great. I'll just have a shower first. Meet you in the kitchen in about ten minutes?"

"Sounds good," James said, and went down the corridor to the kitchen.

As he had expected, there was no-one else there. It was too early for the others on his floor to be up, and those with early lectures or seminars tended to grab a coffee on their way and then delay breakfast itself until ten o'clock, when they ended. Then it was time for a trip to the cafeteria in most cases for a surprisingly decent fried breakfast.

James had made two mugs of tea by the time Adam arrived, his hair still wet from the shower.

"No sugar, right?" James said, putting one of the mugs in front of him as he said down.

"Right," Adam confirmed. "So, everything OK? Why couldn't you sleep? More nightmares?"

James sat down on the chair opposite, thankful for having someone to talk to, but not quite knowing quite where to start.

"Not this time. I Skyped Paul last night," he said.

"It didn't quite turn out the way I expected."

"Why not? What happened?"

"He thinks we should reconsider what we have planned," James said. It sounded clunky and clumsy, but he didn't know how else to say it.

"What does that mean?" Adam asked, and then drank a mouthful of his tea.

"Basically," James went on, "he was worried when I left that it would be the last time we'd see each other as boyfriends. He thought that I'd find someone here, or perhaps even that he would find someone there. But I told him we would still be together when I go back at Christmas. I promised him. I would never cheat on him, or leave him for someone else. He knows that."

"So why does he want things to change?"

"He knows I am struggling here, even though it's only been a couple of days. I want to forget everything that happened back at home, but he knows I can't do that if I'm worrying about him. And he says he's constantly got it on his mind whether we will be together at Christmas. He thinks it will be better for both of us if we act as if we're not an item for the next three months and take some of the pressure off. Then, if I go back home at Christmas and we still want to be together, then we can be, and we haven't lost anything. But in the meantime, he thinks it will be less stressful if we just stay in touch as friends and make up our minds later."

"Leaving you both with the chance to date other people."

"I guess so."

Adam put his mug of tea back down on the table, not sure what he should say to make James feel better, especially as he secretly quite liked the idea of him being free to date others.

"That sounds…complicated," he said.

"Not really, I suppose. I know what he meant."

"But it's not what you want?"

"I wish I *knew* what I wanted. Neither of us have ever been out with anyone else, and while we'd like to stay together, there is that feeling that we should see who or what comes along in the meantime and then make up our minds. We have been together since we were sixteen, and were nearly boyfriends a year earlier than that. It's probably a bit early to pick your partner for life without…"

"Playing the field?"

"I was going to say 'seeing who else is out there.' But yeah, same thing I guess."

"So, did you agree with him in the end?" Adam asked.

"Yeah," James said. "And then I spent all night wondering if I had just thrown what we had away. It just seems so weird. Two years is a long time. I can't imagine not being with Paul. Not really. I guess we'll find out how it works out at Christmas."

"In all likelihood, you'll go back home in December and pick up where you left off. You sound as if you're very close."

"We are, but…"

"It's complicated?"

"It always is, isn't it?"

"Don't ask me," Adam said. "I've never kissed a bloke, let alone gone out with one."

"That sucks."

"It's not something I could think of doing where I live. Everyone knows everybody else's business, and I don't want it getting back to my parents. I know I have to tell them at some point, but I want to be the one who chooses when that is."

James nodded. Although his mum had been fine when he had come out two years earlier, he still would have wanted it to have been at a time of his choosing.

"So, the nightmares," Adam went on, sensing the opportunity to find out more. "What's the story behind them, if you don't mind me asking? You've had one virtually every night since you've been here from what you've said. I'm guessing it's all linked with you not finding it easy away from home, and what happened with your boyfriend?"

"It's a long story, Adam."

"It's half past seven in the morning and I don't have anything to do until 4pm. If you want to tell me, we have all day. But you don't have to. I realise it might be a personal thing that you don't want to talk about. I won't be offended."

James started to tell Adam what had happened when he was at school, and how he and Paul had become boyfriends only for Jason to effectively split them up and exert his power over Paul for the next six months. Then he told him about the night that Paul was turfed out of his own home by his dad and ended up falling off the bridge trying to escape Jason.

Paul had always told James that he had never intended to commit suicide that night, but that he just didn't know what else to do. James wasn't sure if he believed him, even two years later.

Finally, he told Adam about the panic attacks that had started the year before, and the nightmares that had come along at around the same time, and how they were all linked to school in some way. He said that he was planning to go to see the university's counselling service later that day to see if he could get some sessions there like he had back at home.

Adam was a good listener. He didn't try to interrupt, or ask questions, but just let James tell the story his way.

"Thanks for telling me," Adam said, when he finished.

"It's nice for it not to be a secret, to be honest," James said. "I had every intention of leaving all of that behind when I came here. To start afresh. But it's not that easy, it seems. At least now you know why I act a bit strange sometimes."

"You don't act strange! Besides, I'm sure I'll offload on you about my parents at some point, too."

James got up from the chair and went over to the kettle.

"Any more tea?" he asked.

"No," Adam said, "I'm going to head out. I need to

do some shopping. But I'll see you tomorrow night for the party?"

James turned to look at him.

"What party?"

"Oh, shit. Perhaps I forgot to tell you. Some of the others from the floor are having a party tomorrow night in here. The kitchen. They asked us if we wanted to join them, and I said I'd speak to you. But I forgot. I'm sorry."

"It's OK, it doesn't matter. But I'm not really wanting to go to a party."

"Me neither, in all honesty. But they're going to be making a noise anyway, so I'm guessing we might as well go along and see what's going on. They said it won't be much. Apparently, a group of them are in the society for board games, and so they were planning to bring monopoly and trivial pursuit, and that kind of stuff."

"Well, that's better than alcohol and loud music."

"I reckon there'll be that as well."

"Great," James said, sarcastically. "Well, we might as well look in on it then. We can always leave and hibernate in our rooms if we don't like it."

"At least we'll get to meet the others on our floor properly. We might as well get to know who you woke up the other night when you were being murdered."

"Oh, that makes me feel so much better!"

"I'm just kidding. I'll come for you at nine?"

"Yeah, OK," James said. "I'll see you then."

Adam walked to the door and then turned back.

"And make sure you're wearing your best boxers," he said.

"Why?"

"Just in case strip monopoly is a thing."

"Is it?"

"I don't know," Adam said, smiling, and walked back to his room.

2

Jason hadn't been looking forward to poker as much as he usually did. He knew that he had snapped at Mark earlier in the week, and they hadn't really talked since. And then there was the fact that they knew he was now essentially dating Madeline, and there would be various jokes and innuendo about them which he would have to take in good humour whether he wanted to or not. He realised he had probably made a fool of himself when he had snapped at Mark at college, and that Mark was one of those people who would capitalize on it for long after the event.

He also knew that, at some point, he was going to have to finish raising the money for his fees for college. He was still making quite a bit of money through his webcam online, but he now began to feel guilty about basically prostituting himself online to anyone who wanted to watch him get off. He hadn't cared so much before, but now there was Madeline. It made all the difference. How would she feel if she knew? In reality, there wasn't much chance of her finding out by herself, but that was hardly the point. He had already told her a bunch of lies on their first date, and he had added more when she had quizzed him further. Now, whenever he went online he almost felt as if he was cheating on her.

When he was sitting for Madeline earlier in the week, she had asked him to change into some different clothes. When he did, she happened to catch sight of his leg. She must have noticed the fact he had a slight limp and a disfigured leg before, but she had never asked him about it, but now she did.

"What the hell happened to your leg?" she had asked him.

He tried to brush it off.

"Oh, just an accident a few years ago. It's not as bad as it looks."

"What kind of accident?"

Jason had need to think fast.

"On my bike," he said. "There was some broken glass on the road, and I tried to avoid it, but I ended up falling off, and some of it went in my leg."

"Ouch. That must have been horrible."

"It was pretty bad at the time. A few days in hospital."

Jason had continued to get dressed, but knew that, at some point, she would realise that cuts on his leg, even from glass, were unlikely to result in a limp two years later. Jason knew that each lie he told could come back and bite him at some point. He wanted to be honest with Madeline, but he didn't know how to be. Perhaps she suspected that he hadn't been totally truthful with her anyway. Maybe that was why she was asking him about his leg now but hadn't when he had worn shorts in the height of the summer.

He got to the poker game a few minutes late – something he had never done before. When he arrived, only Rick and Madeline were there.

"Hey," he said as Madeline opened the door to let him in. "Sorry, I'm late. Mum was a bit behind with dinner."

Another lie.

"No worries," she said. "We're waiting for Mark anyway."

"Where is he?"

"He's gone to pick up Neil."

Jason had forgotten that a friend of Mark's was joining them for the game. If he had remembered, he might have called up and said he wasn't feeling well. He really wasn't in the mood to be sociable with a friend of Mark's. He just wanted a quiet and relaxing night.

"I finished the drawing," Madeline said, and went over to her folder of artwork and pulled out an A3 charcoal drawing. She showed it to Jason.

"Wow, handsome chap," he said, trying to sound more cheerful than he felt. "And who is this guy?"

"It's you, silly," Madeline said, kissing him on the cheek. "*You're* the handsome guy."

Jason didn't need to be told – dozens of men watching him on webcam two or three nights a week told him the same thing repeatedly. He tried not to take any notice. But he *did* like to hear it coming from Madeline.

"It's great Maddy," he said. "Even better than the last one, I think."

"At the rate she's going, she'll have a portfolio of nothing but drawings of you," Rick said, coming back from the bathroom.

"You're just jealous," she said.

They heard a car draw up outside, and Madeline went over to the window and looked out.

"Mark's arrived with Dickhead," she said.

"You can't call him that," Rick said.

"I don't see why not. If anyone should answer to that name it's Neil."

"Be nice, he doesn't come very often. I think Mark is his only friend."

"Not surprising."

"You only have to put up with him for a couple of hours."

"*Only?*"

"Is this guy really that bad?" Jason asked, just a little intrigued.

"You're about to find out," Madeline said.

She went to the front door and opened it just as Mark and his friend reached it.

"Hey Neil," she said to the newcomer. "Good to see you again."

"You too, Madeline," Neil said, and they embraced somewhat awkwardly.

"I want you to meet Jason," Madeline said. "Neil, this is Jason. Jason this is Neil."

Jason stared at the person who had just walked in, and couldn't believe his eyes. How could this be happening? He got up out of his chair and, rather dazed and with a forced grin on his face, he walked over to shake hands with the person in front of him.

"Pleased to meet you," he said, in the friendliest manner he could.

"You, too," came the reply.

Neil didn't just shake Jason's hand, but squeezed it hard until Jason thought he was going to break some bones. Jason did his best to not let on what had happened.

"Well, I'm just going to use the bathroom, and then we can get on with the game," he said, and left the room quickly.

Jason hurried down the hall into the bathroom, went inside, and shut and bolted the door. He leaned back against it, sweating with panic. Jason had only ever known one person called Neil in his life. Neil Moore. What were the chances that Mark would be friends with him? After everything he had done to try and leave his past behind him, *this* had to happen.

Mark's friend was Badger.

Badger had been part of Jason's inner circle at school. His stooge. He had been made to feel that he was Jason's friend, but he was mostly the butt of his jokes. The last time that Jason had seen or spoken to him, Badger was strapped to a lamppost on the last day of school, wearing nothing but a pair of boxer shorts, and covered in the ketchup, eggs, and flour that Jason and Smithy had thrown over him.

Jason couldn't help but remember the last thing that Badger had said to him as he and Smithy had walked away:

"I'm going to get you, Jason. One day!"

Considering the handshake that Jason had just received, it seemed that Badger had remembered what he had said – and now he had every chance of making that threat come true. Badger could easily spoil everything for Jason by telling Rick, Mark and Madeline all about what had happened at school. And not just about the bullying, but also about how Jason had used and abused his friendship and, more importantly, what had happened with Claire.

Jason washed his face in order to try to cool down, and then took a deep breath before unlocking the bathroom door and going back to the lounge.

"Are we ready to play?" he said cheerfully as he walked in.

"Neil was telling us that you used to know each other at school," Madeline said.

"Yeah, kind of," Jason replied. "We were in the same year, I think. Isn't that right?"

Neil nodded.

"Yeah, that's right," he said, and sat down next to Jason at the table. "It's good to see you again."

3

Jason held the car door open for Madeline, and she got in. When Jason was behind the steering wheel and had closed his own door, Madeline turned to him before he could start the car.

"Before we go anywhere," she said, "what was *that* all about?"

Jason had been tense all evening, constantly worried that Badger (or "Neil," as he was now being called) was going to tell the others about what Jason had been like at school. He had hoped that Madeline hadn't noticed the tension in the air, but now he knew she had. It would have been hard for her to miss it.

"What do you mean?" he said, trying to sound relaxed, and as if he didn't know what she was talking about.

"We might not have known each other for that long, Jason, but I'm not bloody stupid. You and Neil hate each other's guts."

"I don't know what gave you that impression," Jason lied.

"Either you tell me what the hell is going on, or I'm getting out of this car and walking home. I told you last week that people had warned me about you, and I believed you when you said that was it was about a drug problem. But, now, along comes Neil, someone from your school life and his being there clearly scares the crap out of you. And something tells me that *you* used to scare the crap out of *him*, but now he has you by the balls – and I have a feeling that it has nothing whatsoever to do with drugs."

Jason wasn't sure whether Madeline had worked this out for herself, or whether, perhaps, Badger had told her something when Jason was out of the room at some point. Either way, it didn't matter. He was screwed. He now had a choice: bluff his way out of things again and wait for Madeline to find out the truth another time, or just tell her everything and get it over and done with. As he thought about it, kicking the can down the road no longer seemed like the best option. This had to be dealt with now.

"I told you I had a problem with drugs," he said eventually. "That wasn't a lie, really. But my problem wasn't taking them, but selling them. I never took them very much. I tried them, but that's about it. But if you wanted something, pretty much anything, I could have got it for you. I liked the power. I liked the money."

"And what does this have to do with Neil?"

"I haven't finished yet," he said, with more impatience than he intended. "Neil was a friend at school. There was a group of us. But the friendship group fell apart in the last term. And that was my fault."

"Why?"

"We weren't kind to other kids. We bullied them. Just normal stuff that you would expect for most of the time, but in the last year of school something happened. I don't know what it was. And don't ask me why I did it, because I don't know."

"What did you do?"

"There were two boys that we used to take the piss out of. Nothing major, but enough. At the start of our final year at school, we were in a cinema and saw them in the row in front of us, holding hands and kissing. We cornered them. *I* cornered them when we got out, threatened to make their lives a misery. One of them got scared and made out that the other had come on to him. He was lying. We all knew he was lying. We pretended to bring him into our friendship group, but we were never his friend. He was a puppet. He just did whatever I asked him to. For the next six months."

"And that was Neil?"

"God, no. Badger – *Neil* – was already a part of our group. He was doing it, too. He was no angel."

"Why would you do that to those boys?"

Jason would have answered the question if he had known the answer, but he didn't. Even two years on, he had no idea why he had done the things he had. It wasn't just that he now realised the consequences of them, but he had known they were wrong even when he was doing them.

He ignored Madeline's question.

"By the end of the school year, I was out of control. Our group was breaking up. On the last day of term, me and another boy stripped Badg...Neil to his boxers, taped him to a lamppost and covered him in food and stuff. Then we left him there and walked away."

"What were you thinking?"

"I don't know. It was the last day of school. That sort of thing happened all the time. Everyone knew they could get away with whatever they wanted on the last day. It was just a prank that got out of hand. Badger was always the stooge. Not very bright. The one who tagged along."

"Is that everything?"

Jason shook his head.

"Not quite. That night, me and a friend nicked some vodka from home and went out and got pissed. When we were walking home, we found one of the gay kids we had bullied sleeping in an alleyway. He had been kicked out of his parent's house."

"You hadn't told his parents?"

"No. Even we hadn't gone that far. His dad had found out. I don't know who told him. Anyway, we were drunk, and we chased him. We all ended up on the bridge over the river. He thought I was going to beat him up or something, I guess. He panicked, and threatened to jump – and then he fell. I jumped in after him. He had already gotten on to the riverbank safely, but I hit something when I hit the water. Nobody really knows what. That's how I hurt my leg. Nothing to do with a cycling accident. While I was in hospital, it came out in the papers what had been going on at the school – which had a big bullying problem beyond me. But I was at the heart of it and my name was brought up. That's why your friends told you to stay away from me." Jason turned away from Madeline. "They were probably right. You *should* stay away from me."

Jason stopped talking, and waited while Madeline sat quietly for what seemed like an eternity.

"Is that everything?" she said quietly.

"I promise, it is. Something happened that night when I jumped in the river. I suddenly realised what I had been doing. Everything came crashing down around me. My dad turned against me – not that he was around much to start with. I changed, Maddy. You have to believe me. I made sure I have changed. People *can* change, you know? I went and saw the people I had bullied. I apologised to them, as best as I could. I reached out to Claire..."

"Who was Claire?"

"My girlfriend, then ex-girlfriend. I had treated her really badly too. I didn't go and see her, as I didn't think she would want to see me. But I sent her an email saying I was sorry for everything. I have done everything I can to have been good since that night. I'm not lying to you."

"I don't think you are."

"I walked away from all my friends. I knew that I couldn't change unless I did that. I had to get away from them."

"And now one of them turns up at a poker game, and he clearly hasn't forgiven you."

"I don't blame him."

"Neither do I, Jason."

"What are you going to do?"

Madeline opened the car door and got out. She bent down to talk to Jason.

"I'm going to walk home, Jason."

"What about us?"

"I'm going to spend the weekend thinking about that. And I'll let you know next week. Meanwhile, I would suggest you see Neil and try to talk him around. Otherwise, he is going to undo whatever good you *have* done over the last two years. He could ruin your life. For good."

Madeline shut the door, and Jason watched as she walked down the street. He didn't attempt to go after her.

4

Alfred McKechnie hadn't felt well for much of the day.

It had started off with some mild indigestion after lunch, and that, in turn, had given way to him feeling a bit light-headed during the afternoon. The shop had been devoid of customers for much of the day, as it so often was during the week, so he had decided to close for the rest of the day and go home and get some rest. He hadn't been sleeping too well anyway, so had figured that a mid-afternoon snooze would do him no harm.

However, when he had got home, he hadn't been able to sleep. His light-headedness had continued, and he had started to feel hot and sweaty. He missed out dinner altogether because he wanted to neither cook or eat and, instead, had sat himself down in front of the television with a tea-tray on the table beside him. He had loaded up a DVD with a double bill of Sherlock

Holmes films from the 1940s. He knew them inside out, but they were comforting to him, and thought that the sight of Basil Rathbone and Nigel Bruce as Holmes and Watson might take his mind off feeling ill.

Holmes gave his patriotic war-time speech at the end of *Sherlock Holmes in Washington*, and Alfred realised it was probably the one in the series of films he cared least for. The writers had made Holmes rather unlikeable in this one. He went back to the main menu and selected the second film on the DVD: *Sherlock Holmes Faces Death*. He liked this one better – at least it was based on a Conan Doyle story.

He was about to set it running, when he thought he would lock up the house and draw the curtains first. He got out of his chair and went over to the living room window. Across the street, a neighbour was walking down her footpath with a sack full of rubbish to put in the wheelie bin. She saw Alfred at the window and waved to him.

He would have waved back had it not been for a sudden sharp pain in his chest, unlike anything he had experienced before. He knew what it was, and started to panic. He banged loudly on the window, and his neighbour looked across at his house once again, only to see Alfred fall down. She ran into the house to call an ambulance.

CHAPTER EIGHT

1

Badger no longer lived with his parents. Instead, he lived with a couple of friends he had met while he was at college – which surprised Jason when he found out, as he had no idea that Badger had been thinking of going to college after school, that he had been accepted on to a course, or that he was capable of making friends. The only people he had associated with other than Jason back then were a string of girlfriends who normally lasted just a few weeks – although what they had seen in Badger in the first place was something he had never fathomed out. Perhaps it was only Jason's life that had stood still after school.

Madeline had encouraged him to try and sort things out with Badger, and that's exactly what he intended to do. Jason had told Madeline the main facts about what had happened at school, but he had no doubt that Badger would take the earliest opportunity to fill in the gaps in the story – the *really* bad things that Jason didn't want her ever to find out. Like how badly he had treated Claire. He didn't want Madeline to think that she would be treated in the same way.

Jason arrived at Badger's flat around mid-afternoon, but there was nobody home, so he parked the car across the road and waited until Badger arrived. When he saw him walking down the road towards the flat, Jason took a deep breath and got out of the car and shouted across the street to him, and then ran up to him.

"Neil, we need to talk," he said when he had caught up with him.

Neil stopped and turned to face him. He was smiling – a smile that told Jason that this was exactly what he wanted and expected.

"Oh, so I'm *Neil* now, am I? That's strange, because you never once called me Neil at school. But now you want something…"

"It's not like that."

"It's *exactly* like that. I asked you repeatedly not to call me Badger. But you never stopped. Nobody ever stopped. You didn't even think about it. You just carried on as if was one big joke."

"I didn't know you hated it so much."

This wasn't a lie. Jason had no idea that Badger – *Neil* – hated his nickname. He had never once thought that might be the case. Everyone else called him Badger, too. They always had done. He couldn't remember ever being asked to call him Neil, although such a request would probably have resulted in Jason calling him Badger even more, but that was beside the point.

"I'm sorry," Jason said.

His old friend sneered at him.

"Of course you are. Probably the only time you've ever been sorry in your life."

"That's not true, Neil."

"And now you are apologising because you've got yourself a pretty new girlfriend and you don't want me coming along and spilling the beans about what you got up to at school. That's what this is about, isn't it?"

Jason was fast realizing that this was going to be more difficult than he thought. A simple apology about how he had treated Badger – *Neil* - was not going to suffice. This had clearly been planned for some time – certainly before they met at the poker night. No doubt Mark had talked about the new guy at the poker nights and Neil had worked out who it was.

Jason had to try to throw him.

"Madeline already knows about school."

"Like hell she does."

"Ask her if you don't believe me. I told her everything on Friday night when we left the poker game. Then she wouldn't let me drive her home, so she got out and walked. Ask her," he repeated.

Neil stared at him, not quite sure whether to believe Jason or not.

"Look, I'm sorry about how I treated you at school," Jason said. "I'm sorry about everything that happened at school. How I treated everyone. But I'm different now. You have to trust me on that. It's taken me two years to get to where I am now. Please don't mess this up for me."

Neil laughed at him.

"You never cease to amaze me, Jason. Suddenly you think that *you're* the victim. Poor Jason. His new life could be ruined by me. Thick-as-shit Badger. I know what you used to say about me behind my back. Who would have thought that I could screw everything up for you? Times have changed, haven't they?"

Neil turned away from Jason and walked towards the block of flats. Jason didn't know what to do. How was he meant to convince him that he had genuinely changed? That he deserved a second chance? The opportunity to stop this was getting away from him.

"I can't make up for what I did back then," he said to Neil.

Neil turned back to face him.

"No, you can't," he said. "But you didn't care about me then, and I doubt you care about me now, other than how I can screw with *your* life and mess everything up for you. You apologised to everyone, didn't you? I know that. Word gets around. But you didn't apologise to me. Or had you forgotten about that? You probably didn't even realise that you should have done. I never mattered enough."

Jason was silent for a moment.

"I really like Maddy. I don't want to lose her."

Neil walked back down the path towards him.

"I don't blame you. She's nice. Quite a catch. And she likes you, too. God knows why, but she does. *But you left me there, Jason.* Tied to that lamppost on the last day of school. Covered in crap. People took photos. They went all over the web – just like the video you took of James that day in the changing room. But you don't know anything about that, or the comments people left under the photos, because you were in hospital, pretending to be the hero and jumping in the river after Paul."

"I never pretended to be a hero. The papers printed that, but it had nothing to do with me. That day changed my life," Jason said. "It changed me."

"Yeah? That's great. I'm pleased for you. But that day you left me tied up changed *me*. And you need to remember that, because I don't do what you tell me, or even what you ask or beg me, anymore."

Jason took his wallet out of his back pocket. He had been to the cash machine earlier that day, and drawn out all of the money it would allow him.

"I'll pay you," he said to Neil, and took the money out of his wallet.

Neil laughed.

"You think you can buy me? If you think that, Jason, then you haven't changed at all, because buying friendships was what you did at school. With drugs. With power. With threats. Those days are long gone."

With that, Neil walked to the front door of the block of flats and went inside, leaving Jason to worry even more about what Madeline might find out. He feared his visit had caused more problems than it had solved.

2

"Jonathan, you look stressed, my love."

Jonathan looked up from his computer, and saw Miranda standing over him.

Miranda had been at the newspaper longer than anyone else, and despite the sizeable office and the frequent turnover of employees, she went out of her way to act as a mother figure to virtually everyone who worked there – even to the people who were, in fact, older than her, and to the people who had perfectly good mothers of their own. Some thought she was the heart and soul of the office, while others thought she was a busybody who was a total pain in the arse.

"Here," she said to Jonathan. "Have a walnut whip. It will make you feel better."

She held out a box towards him. Jonathan looked at them and smiled at her.

"Thank, Miranda, but I'm allergic to nuts," he said.

This wasn't actually true, but he thought it sounded more polite than telling her he didn't like them.

"That's a terrible thing to be allergic to. A gay man allergic to nuts! Oh, well, I'd better have yours instead then," Miranda said, and bit into one of the sizeable chocolates. "There's no dainty way to eat these things is there?" she said with her mouth full. "You being allergic isn't going to do my figure any good, is it?"

She leaned in towards him.

"So, what's up love?" she said.

"Do I look that bad?"

"You look like shit, love, if you don't mind me saying. Like you haven't eaten in three days, and haven't slept in a week."

"You know how to make someone feel good, Miranda," Jonathan said.

"It's what I'm here for, honey," Miranda replied, completely missing the sarcasm in Jonathan's comment. "So, what's up?"

Jonathan sat back in his chair, and put his hands behind his head.

"Well, I can reassure you that I have been eating properly," he said. "But sleep is another issue altogether."

"No sleep can be a good thing if it's for the right reasons!" Miranda said, winking at him.

Miranda was well-known for inserting innuendo into virtually every conversation.

"Well, in my case, it's because I am sleeping on the couch."

"Oh, no! What's happened? I thought you were happy with your fella?"

"I was. But sometimes things come along and throw a spanner in the works. He's not been well, and not been helping himself either. We had a row, and he's been sleeping in the bed ever since, while I am stuck on the sofa."

"Oh, that's awful, love. What's the matter with him?"

"Mental health stuff. It all dates back to the trouble at the school where he works from a few years back."

"Ooh, that was your big scoop!"

"I'm not sure about that, Miranda."

"Oh, don't be modest," Miranda replied. "That was a huge story, and you know it. It changed things at that school. You should be proud. A more important piece of work than many others in these offices have done."

Miranda was right, and Jonathan knew it, but he wasn't about to take all the credit for it.

"Well, it wouldn't have happened without Andrew. He was the one who put his job on the line to expose what was going on there."

Miranda nodded.

"Yes," she said. "He was quite the hero. You make the perfect couple."

"But the pressure of doing something like that takes its toll," Jonathan went on, ignoring the last remark. "I guess it's bound to. And it's not like he hasn't had issues before. I want to be the good boyfriend and help him through it. But he's not making it easy for me to do that."

Miranda perched herself on the edge of Jonathan's desk and ruffled his hair. He had been the baby of the office when he first started working there – one of the youngest journalists that the paper had ever employed. Miranda still saw him that way, much to his annoyance, although he didn't doubt that her heart was in the right place.

"What are you going to do?" she said.

That was the big question that Jonathan had been asking himself for the last few days. It preoccupied him at work, at home, and in the car. When this had started, there was no doubt in his mind as to what he would do, and what he *should* do. But now he wasn't so sure. He was finding it harder to cope than he thought he would – and Andrew was being more difficult than Jonathan thought he would be. Perhaps this was what he should have expected, but he'd never had any experience of other people with depression or mental health issues. Luckily, his family was devoid of such problems, as far as he was aware. But the way things were with him and Andrew at the moment wasn't helping either of them.

"I don't know what I'm going to do," he said.

Miranda got up from the edge of his desk, accidentally pushing some papers on to the floor.

"Whatever you do will be the right thing – for both of you. I'm sure of it," she said. "Even if it doesn't seem like it at the time."

Then she ruffled Jonathan's hair again, and walked down the office a little further before stopping at another desk and offering the occupant a walnut whip.

3

Earlier in the day, Paul had got a text message from James's mum to say that she was making a cottage pie for dinner, and that she couldn't eat it all by herself. That was her way of letting him know that the house was too quiet and she needed some company. Paul had texted back to say that he would be there at around five o'clock.

He got there a few minutes late, and the pie was already out of the oven and standing on the kitchen worktop.

"You're just in time," Alice Marsh shouted through to him from the kitchen as the front door opened.

Paul didn't need to knock. Alice was regarded as his own mother now. Her house was his house.

"Do you want to eat up the table or in front of the telly?"

"You know my preference on that," Paul said, and reached up to get two lap trays down from the top of the fridge-freezer. He wiped them over with the dishcloth, and then put them down beside her. "How's it going?" he asked her as he did so. "Are you OK?"

She turned and smiled at him.

"Of course I am," she said. "And what about you? Have you settled in to your new place?"

"I guess so. It seems very weird without James here."

"Tell me about it!"

"We always said that we'd get a place of our own. And now we're living miles apart."

"The time will go quickly. He'll be home for Christmas before you know it," Alice said. "How much of this do you want? Are you hungry?"

"I'm always hungry. You know that."

Alice started transferring the pie to the plates in front of her, adding some vegetables from a saucepan as well.

Paul suddenly realised that she hadn't spoken to James since their Skype call when they had decided to "take a break" for a few months. That made things more than just a little awkward. He didn't know if it was his place to tell her, but he thought he should, otherwise he was going to end up lying to her, and he didn't want to do that.

"I spoke with James," he said. "We Skyped each other."

"How is he? Is he settling in OK? He said he'd ring me every day, but I'm lucky to get a text message. Not that I can blame him. I reckon he's busy. First week at university must be quite exciting, don't you think?"

"I guess so. He's doing fine. Still adjusting, I think. He says the bed is too hard. He misses home."

"Well, that's hardly surprising," Alice said. "You're here and he's there."

She passed him his plate of food and he put it on one of the lap trays.

"Things seem so strange," Paul admitted.

"They're going to for a little while."

"We've decided to make some changes."

Just for a beat, Alice stopped serving the food on to her plate. She took a second, preparing herself for what she didn't want to hear, and then carried on with the task.

"Changes? What have you changed?" she asked, trying to sound as if she didn't care or couldn't guess.

"We're…stepping back," Paul said. "Just until

Christmas. I was worried that we wouldn't be together when he came home. And he was worried about me worrying. The whole thing was a mess. And neither of us have ever…"

Paul hesitated, not quite knowing how to put what he wanted to say into words.

"Let's go and sit down, Paul," Alice said, smiling, and they went through into the lounge and started eating.

"What you're basically saying," Alice went on, "is that you have been together since you were sixteen, and you want to make sure you're actually right for each other. You want to know what you're missing."

Paul smiled.

"Not quite like that."

"No, I know. But I think you're right. You've known each other for years, you've never gone out with anyone else, and you don't know anything or anyone else. So, what are you two doing?"

"We're obviously staying in contact. Just like we would anyway. But officially we are just having some time away from being a couple. If we still want to be together when James comes home at Christmas, then that's what we do. But until then, we just take the pressure off both of us a bit."

"You have to do what's right for the pair of you. You're right to ask these questions of yourselves, I think. But never forget that sometimes first love is also true love. It does happen."

Paul nodded, and the pair of them sat quietly eating

their meal.

Alice picked up the television remote control.

"*The Chase* or *Pointless*?" she asked Paul.

"Whichever. I don't mind."

Alice switched on the television, and the pair of them watched as four pairs of contestants struggled to name one book each by the Bronte sisters or Jane Austen.

"He thinks The Pickwick Papers is by Jane Austen?" Alice said rather loudly. "He just said he was a bloody English teacher!"

Paul smiled. He had only moved out a few days earlier, but already he missed living with James and his mum.

"I think you did the right thing," Alice said after a while. "About being together. I think it will do you both good to realise what it's like to be without the other one. It will stop you taking each other for granted when you get back together."

"Thanks."

"And, in the meantime, you can flirt with the guy down the chip shop."

"*You* know about the guy down the chip shop?"

"Paul, *everyone* with a pair of eyes knows about the guy down the chip shop. Who could miss him? If only I was younger."

Yes, Paul certainly missed this.

4

Jason had driven out into the country after he had seen Neil.

He had no clear plan of where he was aiming to go, but just knew that driving for a while might clear his head, and allow him some thinking time on how to deal with his former ally. He needed space to work out what he was going to do next.

He had not expected Neil to stand up to him in the way that he had – he had never had the balls to do so when they were at school. Perhaps things would have been better if he had. Jason had underestimated him, and the fact that other people had changed in the last two years as well as himself. He realised he probably hadn't helped the situation by offering him money to keep quiet, but he so was desperate not to have his new life ruined that he would do anything to stop it. It was only now that Jason realised it made him look like he hadn't changed at all, and that he thought he could buy what he wanted.

There was every chance that it was all going to blow up in his face. Neil seemed determined for that to happen, and, from what Jason could work out, it all stemmed back to the last day of school. So many things did: the humiliation of Neil/Badger; the newspaper article about bullying at school that had resulted in Jason being exposed; and the dive into the river to save Paul, who had gone in only because Jason had left him little choice, or so he had said. All of it happened within a few hours, and they were haunting him two years on.

Perhaps, despite all of his attempts to change, he would deserve it if his efforts of a new life were scuppered by someone from the past.

After an hour of driving, he pulled into a layby and got out and had a smoke before he turned the car around and headed home.

When he went into the house, his mum walked out of the living room to meet him.

"Where have you been all afternoon?" she said to him.

"Out," Jason replied.

"Where?"

"Mum, it's none of your business where I've been." Jason really didn't need an inquisition right now. "But, if you must know, I've been to see an old friend."

"Really."

It wasn't a question.

"Yes, really."

Jason had no idea what the questioning was all about, but he really wasn't in the mood for it. He had told her the truth (or much of it), and she still wasn't happy.

"This came for you this morning in the post," his mum said, holding out a brown envelope. Jason tried to take it from her, but she wouldn't give it to him, holding it up in the air instead. "The return address is the college, and it's easy to see the word 'invoice' through the window on the envelope. So, do you want to tell me what's going on, and where you go every day, or should I just put the pieces together myself?"

Jason couldn't believe it. Everything was crashing down around him. He was well aware that he couldn't keep his enrolment at the college from his parents forever, but he certainly hadn't planned on them finding out so soon. He had at least wanted to prove that he could pay the fees himself, even if it was by earning money in a way he didn't want to, and even felt ashamed of.

Jason snatched the envelope out of his mother's hand.

"I don't think I need to tell you what's going on," he said. "It looks like you've been snooping enough already. I'm surprised you didn't try steaming open the envelope." He turned the envelope over. "Oh, perhaps you already did."

"You were explicitly told that you could not do those arts courses."

"And why is that? You and Dad have never once given me a good reason. You're quite happy for me to doss around the house doing nothing, but you're pissed off when I actually do something constructive. I don't understand you."

"Jason, we haven't understood *you* for years."

"You haven't *tried.*"

"You have everything you want, and this is how you repay us."

Jason walked up the first few stairs towards his bedroom.

"If I had everything I wanted, I'd be at the college

without having to do it behind your back. Giving me money to be a good boy isn't giving me everything I want. I have done all I can over the last few years to turn myself around. You have no idea the amount of people I have apologised to, and how many jobs I have applied for but not got because I'm still remembered as the 'boy from the newspaper.' I have *tried*."

"We want you to go to university."

"I don't want to go to university, Mum."

"You need to do a serious subject."

"That's not who I am. I am not you – and I'm certainly not Dad. That isn't for me. You saw my grades."

"You clearly weren't trying. You could have done resits."

"It wouldn't have mattered! I haven't got it!" Jason said, tapping his head. "Not everyone has. I'm sorry to be such a fucking disappointment."

His mother stared at him.

"You are not to use that language in the house."

Jason laughed.

"After everything, *that's* what bothers you?"

"Your father is not going to be happy when he finds out about this, Jason."

"You know what? I don't give a shit," Jason said. "I'm over eighteen. I can do what I want. It's either this or sitting around the house doing nothing. So, if he's going to hate it so much, don't tell him. You can make that choice, Mum, if you want to. He's hardly at home anyway, so it won't be difficult."

"That's not fair!"

"Lots of things aren't fair, Mum. That's something I'm beginning to realise."

Jason walked further up the stairs. His mum called after him.

"We're not going to pay the tuition fees, you know!"

"I'm paying for them myself, so I don't really care."

"Where are you getting the money from?"

"I'm selling my body!" Jason shouted down the stairs, and then went into his room and slammed the door.

His mum thought it was some kind of joke in poor taste, but as she went back into the lounge, Jason was already booting up his computer to see how much money he could raise for himself by taking his clothes off and wanking on a public webcam. What had been a scary proposition just a couple of weeks earlier had become a daily routine for him.

He wasn't even embarrassed doing it anymore, although he didn't enjoy it either. It was just work, a routine, with the occasional moment of pleasure – sometimes, literally just a moment. He could do what he needed to do on autopilot, and multiple times a day if he needed to.

He always wondered what would happen if he was recognised by someone he knew who just happened to be on the same site at the same time. The chances were slim, but it could happen. But then, they would have to admit they were watching in order to say they had seen him. In the end, it came down to the fact that both of them would be cranking one out, but it was just Jason that was getting paid for it. And Jason certainly wasn't alone in what he was doing, or why he was doing it. He spoke to many other students on the same website who made ends meet in the same way, because grants and loans didn't cover their day-to-day living costs and their families were unwilling or, more likely, unable to help.

On this occasion, at least it would take his mind off everything else that was bothering him. Most people watching would make him feel good by saying how fit he was, or that he was turning them on. Although they could see him, he couldn't see them, and that was probably a plus. Someone who described himself as a good-looking twenty-year-old man could quite easily be obese and seventy in real life, but Jason would never know. At first, he thought he would not be able to cope with the fact that it would be men and not women watching him. Now, it didn't bother him at all. He was fast becoming familiar with the regular visitors to his little corner of the internet, and sometimes he even wondered if these were the only people willing to judge him for what he was doing now rather than what he had done in the past.

5

When James had woken up that morning, it was from

yet another nightmare. He hoped he hadn't woken up the people on his floor again, or they were going to start to get pissed off.

This was a dream where he had logged into Facebook only to find that the video of him in the changing rooms from two and a half years earlier had been posted again, only this time in a group for people attending his university. He had come out of his room to go the kitchen, only to find still images from the video stuck up on the walls of the hallway. When he entered the kitchen, he was faced by the people from his floor, who were huddled around a laptop watching the video and laughing.

He had woken up in a cold sweat, almost unable to believe that the same events had come back to haunt him yet again. He got out of bed and stumbled into the shower. This was normally a brief ritual for him, but today he just stayed under the water, with it beating down on to his head and shoulders. It was almost as if he was hoping that the water would wash the memories of the past from his mind. Getting out from under the shower and then getting dry almost felt like it was too much of an effort to face.

Eventually, he turned the water off, wrapped a towel around his waist, and switched on his laptop. He got himself dry while it booted up, and then he sat down and opened his web browser. Normally, James would check his emails first, but today he went straight to the university's home page, and then found information on the counselling service that was available to both students and staff. He read that he didn't need a doctor's referral, which was going to make things quicker and easier.

He quickly got dressed, made and gulped down a cup of tea, and then headed over to the student support office. He had to get there before he changed his mind.

When he arrived, he was disappointed to see it so full of students. It was only just past nine o' clock in the morning, and so he thought he would have beaten the queues.

He waited patiently in the line for the front desk, and soon realised from what he could hear of the conversations in front of him that virtually all of the other students there were enquiring about getting emergency loans from the university because their student loan hadn't arrived in the bank. When he got to the front desk and explained why he was there, he got directed to a small office at the far end of the building. Other than the secretary behind the desk, there was no-one else there. Perhaps his timing hadn't been bad after all. James spoke to the man behind the desk and explained that he had been having counselling back home and wanted to see if he could continue it while he was at university.

"You were sensible coming here this early in the semester," he was told. "There's hardly any students registered for the service as yet. We should have an appointment for you really quickly. Are you free tomorrow?"

James said that he was, and was booked in for an

appointment in the afternoon.

After he left the office, he went to the campus bookshop to get some of the texts that he would need for his courses that semester. Not all of them were in stock yet, which seemed a little odd to James considering that the start date of term was announced years in advance. Even so, the books they *did* have came to nearly a hundred pounds between them. He stuffed them into his rucksack and headed back to his room.

Lying on the bed, he read a chapter of one of the books he had just bought, which was a discussion of gender issues in Hollywood filmmaking. For the most part, he didn't fully understand what he was reading, and wondered how academic writers could know so much and yet be so unable to explain it in plain English. He got as far as he could, but his mind started wandering, and it was impossible for him to concentrate. When he gave up on the chapter, he put the book down on the floor, pulled the duvet over him, and went to sleep for much of the afternoon. He knew it was going to be a late night due to the party that was going to be held in the kitchen, and so sleeping for part of the day had always been his plan anyway.

Adam knocked on the door at the exact time he had said he would. James hadn't yet known him to be even a minute late.

"Hey," James said, as he opened the door. "You had a good day?"

"Not bad, cheers. You?"

"Yeah. I guess so. Been a bit lazy, to be honest.

Thought I'd have a snooze as I figured tonight might be a late one. Are you ready to do this?"

Adam nodded.

"Of course," he said. "It won't be that bad. But you're going to want to get rid of that jumper, because there's a dozen people in the kitchen, and they have both ovens on for pizza and stuff. It's boiling in there."

This wasn't what James wanted to hear. Not only was he going to have to deal with being sociable with people he didn't know, which was hard enough for him, he was also going to be hot at the same time. If any combination of things was likely to set off a panic attack, it was that. He took off his jumper, and threw it onto the bed, and then he and Adam walked down to the kitchen.

James realised that Adam had clearly been more sociable with the other students than he had let on. He seemed to know everyone's name, and was friendly with them, too. He introduced James to the people in the kitchen, and James seemed to spend the first twenty minutes apologising for screaming in his sleep every night. They all said that they had only heard him on one occasion, but he wasn't sure if they were telling him the truth or trying to make him feel better. It got to the point when, after having the same conversation numerous times, he gave up caring.

The party was considerably quieter than James had expected it to be, at least to start with, and being around lots of others made him forget everything else that was going on – at least temporarily. The mix of board games, pizza and alcohol was oddly enjoyable, despite James's initial reservations about going. Things had got somewhat rowdier towards the end of the evening, when Monopoly was turned into a drinking game, but things never got out of hand, and James didn't play anyway as drinking games really were not his thing.

People started to drift off back to their rooms from about midnight onwards, and Adam and James made themselves a hot drink about an hour later and took it back to their rooms.

James unlocked the door to his room, and held it open for Adam.

"Do you want to drink that in here?" he said to him.

"Sure," Adam replied and follow James into the room. "I need to pee, though."

"You know where the loo is."

Adam went into the small bathroom, leaving the door wide open as he emptied his bladder into James's toilet. James sat down on the bed, and started drinking his mug of decaf tea. Adam came out of the bathroom and sat down beside him.

"Bloody hell," he said as he sat down, "your bed is even harder than mine."

"I think I'm going to spend some of my student loan on a mattress topper," James replied. "Perhaps that way I might get a comfy night's sleep.

"All that alcohol will make you sleep tonight. I thought you said you didn't drink much."

"I don't normally. I just felt like it tonight. I couldn't cope with the drinking Monopoly, though."

"Well, at least we know now that strip Monopoly doesn't exist."

James smiled.

"That's true. I put my best boxers on in case, though, just as you suggested."

"It would have tempted fate if you hadn't. Not that you'd have played anyway, of course."

"Of course. I'm far too innocent for such things. Besides, my Monopoly skills are far too great for me to have been worried anyway."

James watched as Adam flopped back on the bed, his shirt riding up to show off his stomach.

They sat in silence for a few moments. It hadn't been long since James's Skype call with Paul in which they had decided to "take a break" from their relationship, and already he was tempted to make a move on Adam. Here was an Adonis lying on his bed while James himself had drunk more in one night than he probably ever had done before. James finished drinking his mug of tea.

"Perhaps you should go back to your room, Adam," he said.

Adam sat up.

"You want to get some sleep?"

James nodded.

"Yeah," he said. "That might be a good idea. I didn't have much last night."

"OK." Adam got up and went to the door and opened it. "If you have a bad night and you need me, just let me know. I won't mind."

"Thanks, Adam. See you tomorrow."

"Good night,"

"Good night."

Adam walked out of the door, and James closed it, listening as Adam unlocked, and went into, his own room. He sat down back down on the bed, not believing how close he had come to gently placing his hand on the patch of bare skin on Adam's stomach when he had slumped back on the bed.

But he wasn't that guy.

He couldn't be that guy, even after a night of drinking.

James lay down. It had been a close call. He couldn't believe he had even contemplated it, no matter how fleetingly. All of the time he had been suspicious of whether Paul would be faithful, and it had turned out to be himself that was tempted.

But things had changed. And it had been Paul who had changed them.

James got up, left his room, and knocked on Adam's door.

"Give me a second!" he heard Adam shout from behind the closed door.

When Adam opened the door he was wearing nothing but a pair of obviously-tented boxer shorts.

"Shit, Adam, I'm interrupting," James said. "I'll see you tomorrow."

He started to walk back to his own room.

"You don't have to go," Adam called after him.

6

Afterwards, James wasn't sure how he felt about what had happened. After all, it wasn't his idea that he and Paul had taken a break, but he hadn't expected to act on that change of circumstances. At least, not that quickly. But James had needed the comfort of being with someone. Sleeping alone just wasn't an option that night, although sleeping only happened after.

James and Adam were woken by James's mobile phone. He took a few seconds to realise where he was, and to remember what had happened the night before, and then he climbed over Adam to pull the phone out of the pocket of his jeans, which were on the floor. He looked at the screen to see who was calling, and then accepted the call.

"Hey, Mum," he said.

"James. Did I wake you?"

"Don't worry, I probably should have been up anyway."

"I don't know. It's only eight."

"It doesn't matter. What's going on? You don't normally ring this early."

"I wanted to call you because I had some news last night. Are you sitting down?"

"What's going on?"

"Alfred is in hospital. He's had a heart attack."

"Shit. Is he OK?"

"From what I can gather, yes. It was just a minor one. They're keeping him in for a few days – you know, for observation."

"I'll come home to see him."

"There's no need, James. He's got his phone with him, you could call him."

"Mum, if Alfred is in hospital, then I'm coming home to visit him. You know that."

"I do. But I promised Alfred I would try to stop you. And I tried."

"Not very hard."

"That's beside the point."

"When did it happen?"

"The night before last, at his home. Luckily, he was drawing his curtains at the time and a neighbour saw it happen, so he got help really quickly."

"That's good."

When he ended the call, James explained what had happened to Adam.

"I have to go home. I don't know how long I'll be gone."

"I hope your friend will be OK."

"Me, too. And I have to meet my boyfriend, too. That could be awkward."

"We didn't do anything. And he was the one who wanted you to have a break. You had a wank. That's all. I didn't even really touch you."

"I know, I know. It's just...weird."

James got out of bed and got dressed. He quickly said goodbye, and then went to his room to look up the times of the trains home.

CHAPTER NINE

1

Andrew sat in the doctor's office and told her straight out:

"I want to go back to work."

He hadn't planned to go back to see the doctor so soon, and only managed it because someone had cancelled an appointment just before he had called. And he certainly hadn't been thinking about returning to work until the previous day, when he had come to the sudden realisation that perhaps getting back into a routine might be good for him. He also figured that it couldn't make him feel any worse, and that things couldn't deteriorate any more at home, either.

Jonathan was still sleeping on the sofa, and he and Andrew still weren't talking to each other besides the occasional "good morning" and "I'm going to bed." Andrew was well aware that one more wrong move on his part could result in Jonathan simply moving out and staying with his mother instead – and, if that happened, he doubted that his boyfriend would ever come back. Why on earth would he want to?

Andrew had no idea how long the renewed energy he was feeling would last, but he was hoping that it was a change for the better, and perhaps a permanent one brought about by the increased dosage of his medication. He felt that he might have finally broken through "the wall."

The doctor that sat across from him seemed less convinced.

"I'm not sure that would be such a good idea at this point, Mr. Green," she said.

"What do you mean?"

"It was only a week ago that you were here in my office, and clearly unwell, and almost unable to function at all."

"But I'm feeling better now."

"I am sure you are, and I am glad that is the case. But people don't get better from this kind of thing overnight. I would suggest that you make the most of this current improvement. Start getting into a routine around the house. Go out, and see how much you can do without getting overly tired. See friends, go shopping, go to the cinema if you want to."

Andrew couldn't believe what he was hearing. He was feeling better, and all the doctor could suggest was that he went out to see a film? How would that look if other teachers or kids from the school saw him? He would look and feel like a fraud. He was worried that his work colleagues were thinking he was not really ill as it was. In fact, quite the opposite was true, and many had been worried about his health for several months but hadn't quite known how to approach the subject.

"I want to go back to work," he said again.

"I'm sorry, Mr. Green. That is not something I am willing to agree to. You have a fit note stating that you should not to return to work for a month. That means you cannot return to work without another note from me to say that you can. I am not willing to write that at this stage. It's not in the interest of yourself or the school. When you *do* go back, I would suggest that you do so on a part-time basis for the first few weeks. That is something you can be proactive about now, if you would like to. You could raise this issue with the school and see if they would be willing for you to return part-time in the first instance. But it isn't going to be for a few weeks."

"Are you saying that I am going to get worse again?"

"I am saying that depression is unpredictable, and while you might feel well today – and that is a good sign – you may not feel as well tomorrow. That's why we need to wait for a sustained improvement rather than jumping the gun. I realise that might be frustrating. I'm sorry."

It *was* frustrating, but when Andrew left the medical centre, he also realised that the doctor had spoken sense, no matter how much he hated to admit it. It *had* only been a day, after all. So, he would do what he could to improve the broken relationship with

Jonathan. Perhaps he would start by cooking a meal for dinner. At least he had some appetite back, which meant there was unlikely to be a repeat of the mealtime from a few nights earlier when he could barely eat a mouthful. Cooking dinner was at least a start.

2

"Are you coming to poker night?"

The text appeared on Jason's mobile phone via Facebook Messenger. Madeline had sent it.

Jason was glad to get a message from her - and surprised. He had been in two minds whether to go to the poker game or not. On the one hand, he was desperate to try to smooth things over with Madeline, and it would give him the perfect excuse to see her, but, on the other, he had little appetite for being quizzed about the atmosphere that had occurred the previous week. It wasn't as if Madeline would have been the only one to have noticed it.

"Do you want me to?" he texted back.

He already knew the answer. She wouldn't have asked him if he was going if she didn't want to see him. That was a good sign. Perhaps things would work out fine after all, especially if Neil didn't go any more. But what would happen when he did? Jason didn't even want to think about having to sit there with him again.

Just a week earlier, everything had been going so

well for Jason. It really had looked like he and Madeline would finally get together, and then along came Neil (and Jason still couldn't get used to referring to him by that name) to screw everything up. And then that was followed by his mother finding out about his enrolment at college. How could things fall to pieces so quickly?

Jason still hadn't been able to ascertain whether his mum planned to tell his father about college. Whenever he took her aside and asked her, she refused to give a concrete answer, telling him to "wait and see," or that she would make up her mind later but wasn't in the habit of lying to her husband. It was almost as if she was enjoying making Jason wait to find out what would happen.

Jason found it a little ironic that his mum didn't want to lie to her husband given how often he thought his dad lied to his mum. The "business trips" had become so frequent that Jason was beginning to doubt whether they were for business at all. He kept telling himself that his dad finding out about art college wouldn't change anything. His parents weren't paying for the tuition in the first place, although they could, theoretically, stop giving him money of any kind, and that would cause a significant problem. That was, after all, the money that Jason was living off. He still thought he could raise the cost of the fees himself, but living expenses were another thing altogether.

Jason's phone vibrated to signal another message.

"Yes. You need to be there. Nothing is going to get better if you hide away."

Madeline was right, of course. She already knew most of the story, but Rick and Mark only knew whatever Neil had told them. If Jason had really changed over the previous two years, then he had to prove it to them and face up to what he had done in the past.

"OK," he texted back. "I'll be there at the usual time. Might be awkward, though,"

"You've got to do it sometime," the reply came back. "You might as well do it now. Xx."

Jason put the phone back in his jeans pocket, and then headed for the shower. If he was going to see Madeline, then he had to look his best.

3

The journey home seemed never ending.

The train had been nearly an hour late when James had got on it, although no-one seemed to know why, and by the time it arrived at its destination, it was more than an hour behind time. There was nowhere on the train to get a drink or something to eat, the toilet was blocked, and the wi-fi wasn't working – not that it ever seemed to work on a train anyway, despite posters all over the carriage walls telling passengers it was free. James *did* manage to get enough phone signal to ring up the counselling service at the university in order to cancel his appointment for later that day, but, other than that, it was an infuriating few hours, especially when he was desperate to find out how Alfred was.

When he finally arrived, he felt the station was almost welcoming him home. It was good to be back in familiar surroundings, even if the reason for his return wasn't a pleasant one. James didn't hang around. Instead, he got out of the station as quickly as he could, and hopped into a taxi to the hospital. He could have gone home first, but he knew he wouldn't relax until he had seen Alfred.

When James finally found the right ward after getting lost within the maze of hospital corridors, he was pleased to see that Alfred was sitting up in bed and somewhat reluctantly eating some rather mushy-looking food on the plate in front of him. His face lit up when James walked in.

"Master James!" he said, smiling broadly. "I told your mum not to get you back here on my account. You're meant to be away enjoying yourself."

"You know me better than that, Alfred," James said, sitting down in the chair beside the bed. "I wasn't going to know you were in hospital and not visit."

"Well, I'm glad you're here, all the same. It's good to see you, my boy."

The old man didn't *look* like he'd had a heart attack. In fact, James thought he looked better than he had done for some time.

"Mum said it was a heart attack," he said. "Is that still what they think it was?"

"Apparently," Alfred replied. "But a minor one. A

warning that I need to slow down, so they say – although how I can get around any slower than I do already, I have no idea. You're not going to get rid of me just yet, apparently."

"Pleased to hear it. How are you feeling now?"

"As good as new, to be honest with you. I want to go home, but they won't let me. Miserable buggers. A few more days, they're saying. It has been all rather scary, though, I'll tell you that. I thought that me and Sherlock Holmes were going to be parted forever – or perhaps reunited somewhere, not that I believe in all that claptrap, of course. Talking of which, that volume you gave me before you left is beautiful. Thank you."

"No problem. I was going to hang on to it until Christmas, but thought better of it."

"I left it in the shop. Would you be good enough to go to the shop for me, now that you are back? There really should be a note on the door saying it will be shut until further notice, or something like that. You know the kind of thing – not that I am sure that anyone will care whether it's open or not. And pick up my complete Sherlock Holmes book and bring it to me here, will you? I feel lost without it. Would you mind?"

"Not at all, Alf. I'll do it later this afternoon, and bring the book in this evening."

"There's a good lad."

Alfred put his fork down, and pushed the plate of food away. He leant forward towards James.

"The food in here is bloody awful," he whispered.

"It looks it," James whispered back. "What is it?"

173

"Damned if I know. Cottage pie, or so it said on the menu. Doesn't look much like cottage pie, though. I think they forgot to put the mince in. Can't complain, though. I don't know how the old NHS keeps ticking over, all things considered, with what the bloody Tories have done. And I doubt things are about to change. They're all the same, these bloody politicians. But the people here saved my life, young James. I know that for a fact. I don't envy the doctors and nurses, working all the hours God gives, and for not much money, but they are miracle workers, I know that for certain – although I'm sure one of the nurses keeps flirting with me!"

"Is she good-looking?"

"It's a man!" Alfred, said, winking at James.

"You must point him out to me!"

Alfred laid back in the bed and closed his eyes. James wondered if he was going to fall asleep.

"I thought I was a gonner, Jim-lad," he said, his eyes still closed.

"I'm glad you weren't."

"But it has got me thinking. I don't know if I will open the shop again. Perhaps I'm just getting too damned old. Shops like mine are an endangered species. And I'm nothing but an old worn-out fossil. Perhaps I'm an endangered species, too." Alfred opened his eyes, and grinned. "But I reckon I'll change my mind on that once I escape from this place!" he added. "And what about you? Tell me all about university. Are you enjoying yourself? Or rather, *were* you enjoying yourself until this old fart had a heart attack and brought

174

you home!"

James didn't know what to say. He knew that Alfred really wanted him to enjoy university, and had told him numerous times that it was the start of his new life. James didn't want to disappoint him. But he couldn't lie either. Not to Alfred.

"I don't know," he said. "I'm struggling at the moment. I miss home, and Paul, and Mum. And you. And the shop. Things have got tricky with me and Paul already. But I just don't feel settled there yet. I suppose it's too early to expect to."

"What are the other students like?"

"I've made friends with the boy who lives in the room next door. He's really nice."

"I'm sure it will get better for you," Alfred said. "These things take time. Change always does. But sometimes change is for the better, no matter how much we think we don't want it. And you tell me you're struggling there, but I also know that you were struggling *here*, too."

James stared at him.

"What do you mean?"

"How long have I known you? Three years? Four? You're like a grandson to me, and I know when you're not happy. Master James, I don't care whether you're here at home, at university, or on the other side of the world – as long as you're happy. You deserve to be happy."

"Thank you, Alfred," James said.

"But now I need some sleep." Alfred put his hand

on James's. "So, will you go to the shop for me and do what I have asked?"

James said that he would.

"When are you going back to university?" Alfred asked.

"I don't know. Probably after the weekend. Trying to travel by train at the weekend is a pain with all the replacement buses due to rail repairs. I can't be bothered with all of that. I've just got to tell my advisor at university how long I will be away for. Not that I have met him yet. But you'll see me over the weekend."

"Hopefully I'll be home by the time you go back, then."

"I hope so, Alfred."

Alfred smiled, closed his eyes again, and drifted off to sleep.

4

James got a big hug from his mum as soon as he walked through the door. He had expected it, but took the time to remind her that he had only been gone a week.

"You look thin," she said.

"I haven't got thinner in a week."

"I told you to eat well while you were at university."

"I have been eating, Mum. I promise."

"Yes. Baked beans on toast, no doubt."

"Student cuisine has developed considerably since the days of baked beans on toast every day, Mum. I'm not starving or eating unhealthily."

"Hmmm. Well, you'll have a proper meal tonight, at least. How long are you home for?"

James shrugged his shoulders.

"I don't know yet," he said. "I haven't made my mind up. But I'll be here for the weekend, I guess. I don't fancy travelling back on Sunday. You know what the trains are like on a Sunday."

"I don't blame you. About time they sorted that out. It's been going on for years. Tea?"

"I'd love one."

James and his mum walked into the kitchen, and he sat down on a stool and watched while she filled up the kettle.

"Paul came for tea yesterday. It was good to see him," Alice Marsh said. "It's been quiet here since you've both gone. The house has been so empty, especially with both of you leaving at the same time. I think he's settled into his new flat, though. Paul told me about your…change in circumstances."

James felt that Paul shouldn't have done. His mum was struggling with him being at university without having anything else to worry about.

"I wish he hadn't," James said.

"Why?"

"Because you'll worry."

"I worry anyway, so it doesn't make much of a difference. I don't think what you've done is such a bad idea, anyway. Perhaps you *do* both need a bit of time away from each other, just to make sure you've made the right decision."

"Maybe," James replied, knowing full well that he wasn't going to tell her about the events of the night before with Adam. She and him were close, but they weren't close enough to share those kinds of details.

They took their mugs of tea through to the lounge and sat down.

"So, have you been to the hospital already? How is Alfred," Alice asked.

James sipped his tea. Why did something as simple as tea taste so much better in the comfort of your own home and with your own mug?

"He's OK. They've told him it was only a minor heart attack, and that he'll be able to go home in a few days. He's already complaining that he can't go home now. He's so independent and stubborn. He wants me to go to the shop and pick up a book and take it to him. I'll do that this evening. They have visiting until eight o'clock, so there is plenty of time."

"That's good news. Perhaps we can find some food you can take to him. Hospital food isn't great."

"I saw some of it today. It looks disgusting. Didn't look much like shepherd's pie to me."

James had some more of his tea.

"I think he's going to close the shop, Mum."

His mum put her hand on his shoulder.

"You've spent a lot of time there."

James nodded, close to tears.

"You can't blame him, though," his mum went on. "These health things come as a wake-up call that you can't carry on as you once did. He's not getting any younger – and I doubt that place even covers its own costs these days. That's even more worry for him. It probably could if he made use of the internet, but that's not Alfred's way, is it?"

James shook his head.

"Nope, and he's not going to change. It's like asking him to read Sherlock Holmes on a Kindle. It ain't going to happen."

James's mum decided to change the subject.

"How are you getting on at university?" she said.

It was the question that James was dreading. The truth of the matter was that he was not happy, and the more he thought about it on the train home the more unhappy he had become. He had spent the summer looking forward to it so much, but now that he was there, all he wanted to do was come home. He was pleased to have met Adam, and knew he was lucky to have him in the room next door, but that didn't solve the fact that James felt alone and vulnerable. One friend was never going to take the place of a mother and a boyfriend.

At the same time, he knew that he wasn't ready to give up on it already. He *did* want to be at university, but at the same time, he was wondering whether this was the right time for him to go. Perhaps he should have waited until he had his head sorted out – until the nightmares had stopped. He was beginning to think he should have asked for a deferred entry to the following year. He had spent much of the train journey home wondering if it was too late for that to happen. But the semester was only a week old. He was tempted to write an email to find out. But he was scared that, if he gave up now, he would never go back the following year or at any time.

"I'm struggling, Mum," he said.

His mum put her hand on his.

"What's the matter?" she asked. "Are you homesick?"

James shook his head.

"Honestly, Mum, I don't know. It just doesn't feel right for me. Not now."

They sat in silence for a few seconds, before Alice said:

"You don't *have* to go back. You know that, don't you? I'm not going to think badly of you if you decide this isn't right for you. No-one is. People just want you to be happy."

James smiled.

"I know," he said, and then put his arms around his mum, and started crying.

5

Jason was concerned that poker night would be some kind of ambush. He was worried that he might turn up only to find Badger there after all, ready to gloat while he told the others what an arsehole Jason had been when he was at school.

There was no sign of Badger, for which Jason was thankful, but the dynamics of the group had changed, nonetheless. Madeline and Rick tried to act as if nothing had altered, although their acting abilities left something to be desired. Mark, on the other hand, made no pretense. Badger had told him everything – Jason was sure of it, and Mark was determined to make the most of the information. It was clear from the smirk that greeted Jason as he walked into the flat.

At one point, when Jason raised the bet, Mark turned to him, and said:

"You never raise. It's almost as if you have something in your hand that you want to tell us about."

When Jason threw his cards down on the table after losing a hand, he was asked:

"Things not going your way? You must have some sins of the past coming back to bite you on the butt."

Jason wanted to either punch him or just get out of there as quickly as possible, and he wasn't sure which option he preferred. At one point, he nearly bet all of his chips on a hand that he was never going to win just so that he could have an excuse to leave. But he still had a fighting instinct, and if this was going to be the last game of poker that the four of them played (and he had resigned himself to the fact that it probably would be), he was planning on winning it if he possibly could.

Madeline tried her best to make Jason feel more

comfortable. She smiled at him as she always did, touched his hand, and even rubbed her foot up his leg under the table. Jason thought that there still might be some hope of them staying together when everything had blown over, but he also knew that, while she clearly didn't hate him, she was disappointed in him. And he couldn't blame her for that; he was disappointed in himself.

Eventually, Jason lost the last of his chips and limped out of the game.

"You didn't seem to be concentrating so much tonight, Jason," Mark said. "Perhaps you had something else on your mind."

The room went quiet.

"The only thing I had on my mind, Mark, was beating you," Jason replied.

"To a pulp?"

Mark was hardly known as the most quick-witted member of the group, and his quips were normally sex-related, which was what his mind seemed to be obsessed with, and Jason was taken aback by the comment.

"What do you mean by that?" he asked.

Mark held up his hands.

"Nothing. Nothing at all, Jason. Just a joke."

"Sure."

An uneasy silence prevailed for a few seconds.

"By the way," Mark said eventually, "Neil told me to tell you that Claire says hello."

Jason stared at him.

It was clear that Mark had been waiting all evening

to say it, even if it was doubtful that he actually knew what he was talking about beyond the knowledge that it would make Jason angry or nervous. Or both. Neil had obviously put him up to it. Jason could just imagine him telling Mark to say the words and to watch the fireworks, but Jason was determined not to fall into that trap.

"Well, tell him to tell her that I said hello back, Mark," he said, smiling. "I hope she's happy. I didn't realise that Neil was in contact with her."

"Oh, they're in *regular* contact, if you get my meaning," Mark said. "They have been for a year or so."

Jason couldn't believe it.

"They're going out with each other?"

"Oh yes," Mark said. "I thought you knew."

Mark clearly knew that Jason *wasn't* aware of this latest bombshell. If Neil and Claire were an item, then she might have told him everything about what had happened between them – maybe stuff that she hadn't told anyone else. Jason was suddenly aware that Madeline was eventually going to find out how he had treated Claire unless he did something to stop it soon.

Jason was beginning to believe that this was what he deserved. Perhaps it was just fate. The way he had treated Claire had been awful. If Madeline found out now, as it seemed she was bound to, at least it would stop him treating her in the same way.

Jason stood up.

"I think I need to go," he said. "I'll see you all at college. Probably."

"You're not going to wait so you can give me a lift?" Madeline asked him.

"Not tonight, Madeline. I'm sorry."

He took his jacket off the back of the chair and walked out of the flat, knowing he was never likely to ever go back there.

He got into the car, and sat behind the wheel, literally shaking. He tried to light a cigarette, but only succeeded in dropping it onto the floor. He punched the steering wheel and screamed out in fury. It was what he needed. A release.

He took a few minutes to pull himself together so that he could drive. He looked back at the flat he had just left. He saw the blinds move in the window, and then the door to the block of flats opened and Madeline started walking down the footpath towards the car. Before she could reach him, he quickly started the car and drove off.

6

Jonathan arrived home from work later than usual. His lateness was intentional.

Andrew greeted him as he walked in the door.

"Hey," he said, clearly a little uncomfortable at making the first move to reconciliation.

"Hi," Jonathan replied, not sure of what to make of Andrew's sudden interest in talking to him. This current interaction had already been roughly the same length as most of their conversations over the previous few days.

"How was work?" Andrew asked.

"Good, thank you. I had to stay late to finish something I was writing."

That wasn't strictly true, but Jonathan had been in no hurry to get home for another evening of the silent treatment from Andrew. Quite the opposite in fact.

He suddenly realised that he could smell food.

"Have you been cooking?" he asked.

"Yeah, I thought I should do something other than sit around the house all day."

Jonathan was about to say that it was about time, but thought better of it. Cooking was at least a step in the right direction.

"Yours is in the oven, keeping warm," Andrew went on. "It might be a bit dry by now, but it's there if you want it."

"Thanks. What did you cook?"

"Casserole."

Jonathan had brought home a take-away, but was more than happy to bin it if it meant giving Andrew a morale boost by eating what he had taken the time to cook.

"I'll go upstairs and get changed, and then I'll have it," he said.

"Cool," Andrew said, and followed his boyfriend upstairs, watching from the bedroom doorway as he got changed. "I put some washing in the machine today. I saw you were getting short of shirts for work. They were mounting up. I'll do some ironing tomorrow."

"You have been busy."

"Yeah. I woke up feeling better this morning. I don't know why."

"Perhaps the tablets are kicking in."

"Maybe. I don't know. I went back to the doctor's today, too. I wanted to know if she would let me go back to work."

Jonathan tensed up a little. Andrew doing stuff around the house was probably a good sign, but him wanting to go back to work at this stage just seemed a little bizarre.

"What did she say?" he asked.

"She said I wasn't ready for it yet. One good day didn't mean that I was ready for that kind of commitment, according to her."

Jonathan gave a sigh of relief.

"She's probably right, Andy," he said.

"Yeah, I guess. But she said I should contact the school at some point anyway, and see if they would be willing for me to go back part-time in the first instance. Just to ease me back in."

"That sounds sensible," Jonathan said as he pulled a T-shirt over his head.

"Yeah. I thought so too. But apparently even that won't happen for a few weeks."

"Well, the school made it clear that you had to be fully fit before you went back. You can't blame them for that. You already left a class unattended. They have to look after their own interests too."

Andrew knew that all too well, but the sudden burst of energy was making him frustrated to be at home.

"Yeah, I know," he said. "I'll make the most of the time at home instead. I thought I might try and come up with some new ideas for lessons rather than just repeating what I've been doing for years. I think I might have been getting a bit stale. I should try a new start when I eventually go back."

This sounded like a positive move to Jonathan.

"That's a good idea, I think. Now, let's go and get this food out of the oven."

"You can have your take-away if you want. I know you bought one. I can smell it."

"You took the time to cook, so I'll eat it," Jonathan said, and, for the first time in several days, he kissed his boyfriend and then went downstairs.

7

Just a few minutes after leaving the poker game, Jason stopped the car outside Claire's parent's house. He was hoping that she was there alone. There was no car in the driveway, so it seemed likely that neither her parents or Badger were there. The big question was whether Claire herself was at home.

Jason had not had any intention of going to see Claire that evening, but the idea had come into his head as he drove away from poker game, and just decided to go with it. He was at the stage where he could hardly make things worse. Getting out of the car before he lost his nerve, he walked up the path to the front door, and rang the bell. A few seconds later, he heard Claire's voice from behind the door. It was strange hearing her voice again.

"Who is it?" she asked.

Jason took a deep breath.

"It's Jason," he said.

There was a pause for a few seconds.

"What do you want?"

"I need to talk to you."

"I don't think that's a good idea."

"Claire, please. Just this once. Let me talk to you. I'm begging you."

There was another pause, and then Jason heard the door being unlocked. The door opened, and Jason saw Claire for the first time in two years.

"Hey," he said.

"Hi, Jason."

"You look well."

Jason wasn't lying. She was wearing an old pair of pyjamas that looked as if they were ready to fall to pieces, but she looked different to when he had last saw her. Older, of course, but more confident, too. As with Badger, two years had changed her a lot.

"What do you want, Jason? You shouldn't be here."

Jason smiled. She had never had the guts to speak to him in that tone of voice before. He was beginning to wonder if he had done the right thing by coming to see her, but he wasn't about to walk away now.

"I'm sorry, Claire," he said. "For everything."

Claire stared at him. Jason could see that she was trying to work out what to say.

"You told me that in your email two years ago."

"But you need to believe me. I mean it."

Claire stepped out of the house and pulled the door to behind her. She clearly had no intention of asking Jason inside.

"Jason, I *do* believe you. But that doesn't mean I want to see you. Or that I want any contact with you."

"But I treated you so badly. That night…"

"Yes, you did. You were a pig. A thug, almost. You hurt me. Not just physically. But I still came back for more. I was an idiot. I was naïve, and stupid. And so, probably, were you. But it's over now. I've moved on, and you've moved on, so let's just leave it behind us. I'm sorry I didn't reply to that email, but I was still raw then. I'm not now. And I thank you for apologizing. I'll never forgive you, Jason, but I have no intention of letting what happened rule my life two years later."

This wasn't the response that Jason was expecting. It didn't even sound like Claire talking. If only she had been like this when he was going out with her.

"Neil told me he saw you, and that you're doing OK. College, he said," Claire went on. "He said you've started over, and tried to make something of yourself. I'm really pleased, Jason. You were a bastard, I'm not going to lie about it, but it takes a lot to admit what you did, and to try to start again. Neil's pleased for you, too.

I know he is."

Jason stared at her. She didn't have a clue about what her current boyfriend was doing, and how he was trying to ruin everything for him. Jason had come to see Claire in order to beg her to try to stop what Badger was doing, but he couldn't do that now. He wasn't going to be the one to tell her that her boyfriend was being an arsehole and trying to ruin his life, although he knew it would be far better for her in the long run if he did.

"Thanks, Claire," he said. "Thank you for seeing me. I hope everything goes well with Neil."

"Thanks, Jason," she said. "I'll tell him you popped around."

"Yeah. Do that," Jason said. "I look forward to seeing him again soon."

Jason said goodbye, got in his car and drove off, much happier than he was earlier in the evening.

When he got home, he wasn't concentrating on what he was doing. He parked the car in the driveway, and accidentally bumped into the garage doors as he did so. The damage wasn't much, just some damage to the front bumper, but Jason didn't care. He only had to deal with Badger, not Claire, and, if all else failed, he'd threaten to tell Claire what her boyfriend was doing. Two could play at that game.

When he got inside, he went up to his room and texted Madeline, apologising for leaving so suddenly. He told her that everything was going to be sorted soon, joking at the end of the message that he had been an idiot and damaged the front of the car while parking.

8

After he had eaten, James went to Alfred's shop to put the notice on the door and to pick up the book of Sherlock Holmes stories. When he got to the hospital, he found that Alfred was asleep. James didn't want to wake him, and so left the book with a nurse, who promised to pass it on when he awoke.

Half an hour later, James found himself inside Paul's flat for the first time. They hugged silently for a few seconds when Paul opened the door and let him in.

"It's good to see you," Paul said, as he went into the kitchen area. "Although it sucks about what happened to Alfred. How is he?"

"He was fine when I saw him this afternoon. I just popped a book in to him, but he was asleep. The nurse says she'll pass it on. I didn't think it would be the right thing to do to wake him."

"Sherlock Holmes?"

"What else!"

"I'm glad he's going to be OK. Tea or beer?"

"You've got the fridge stocked up already, have you?" James said, smiling.

"Yep."

"Beer. I think I could do with one." James said. He looked around the flat while Paul got the drinks from the fridge. "This looks nice. Quite homely."

"Yeah, small though," Paul said, handing him the drink.

"It's massive compared to my room at uni."

"Yeah, I saw it on the webcam. I don't think I could cope with living in a room that small."

"I struggle. How do you like having your own place?"

"I don't know. Ask me in a month. I went to your mum's for tea and realised how much I missed the company."

"I'm sure she misses you, as well. I miss having her around, too."

James opened his can and took a mouthful.

"I signed up for counselling at the university as you suggested, by the way," he went on. "I had an appointment for today, but obviously had to cancel it. They said I should be able to rearrange it for next week."

"Good. I'm sure it will help."

"I hope so."

"When are you going back?"

"Monday, I guess."

"You don't sound too enthusiastic."

"I'm not. It will get better."

Things were clearly awkward between them. Neither of them ever thought that they would be seeing each other for the first time in a week and just sitting down to engage in small talk. But that was what had come from their change in status, which had possibly been decided rather too hastily during the webcam chat. They were both beginning to realise that might be the case. And there was the small matter of what James had done the night before. He couldn't keep it to himself any longer. James didn't know if he should mention it or not, but he had to tell Paul.

"I need to tell you something," he said.

"Adam?"

James nodded.

"That didn't take long for you to work out. You're obviously not surprised."

"You looked so miserable when we chatted. And lonely. There is a good reason why I suggested that we hold off on things till Christmas."

"We went to this party last night. Just the people from our group of rooms at uni."

"What happened?"

"We said goodnight. And he went to his room and I went to mine. About ten minutes later, I realised I wasn't going to be able to sleep, so wanted to see if he might want to, I don't know, watch some TV or something. But we didn't watch TV."

"What did you do?"

"Nothing we couldn't have done alone. We didn't even touch each other, I promise."

James wasn't sure how Paul was going to take this news.

"I don't care," Paul said.

James wasn't sure if Paul not caring was a good or a bad thing.

"Why?"

"Because if you were really into this guy, and he was some threat, you wouldn't have told me."

"I would have."

"But not in that way."

"No, probably not."

"So, why don't you stop feeling guilty and stay here for the night?"

James wanted to say yes. He really wanted to sleep with Paul's arms wrapped around him, making him feel safe from the things that troubled him whenever he seemed to shut his eyes.

"Tomorrow?" he said. "I haven't slept properly all week. I just need to catch up on sleep first. Then we can have the rest of the weekend. Is that OK?"

"Of course."

The conversation became easier after that. James talked about the people he had met at the university, and the societies he had joined. He tried to sound enthusiastic, but wasn't sure if he was fooling Paul.

Two hours later, they kissed each other goodnight, and James said he would come around the following morning. As he walked down the road, James heard a message come through on his phone. He took it out of his pocket. It was from Paul.

"I've missed you," it said.

James smiled to himself and put the phone in his pocket. Perhaps things would be alright after all.

James wasn't paying attention when he stepped off the pavement onto the road at the pedestrian crossing, and so didn't see the speeding car coming towards him.

The next thing James knew, he was in an ambulance.

CHAPTER TEN

1

Alice Marsh received the phone call at just after eleven o'clock in the evening while she was watching *The Graham Norton Show* and having her last cup of tea and a biscuit before bed. Daniel Radcliffe was chattering away, telling a funny story about working with Maggie Smith, and the audience were laughing, but Alice wasn't really concentrating. She was worried about her son.

As soon as she heard the phone ring, she knew that it was bad news. Nobody would ring her that late under normal circumstances, and James would have just texted her if he had decided to stay at Paul's overnight – something which she had expected to happen.

Perhaps it would be a wrong number.

She picked up the phone with trepidation.

"Hello?"

"Hello. Could I speak to Alice Marsh, please?"

"Speaking."

"I am sorry to call you so late. I am calling from St. Celia's Hospital. The A&E department. You son has asked me to call you."

Strangely, Alice's first reaction was relief. She couldn't help it. If James had asked the nurse to phone, then he must be alive and able to talk. Then followed those dreaded words, "I'm afraid there's been an accident."

By the time Alice ended the call, she was shaking. She knew that the news could have been much worse. James had been knocked down by a car in a hit-and-run. Miraculously (that was the word used by the nurse), his injuries were relatively minor. He was then about to be taken for X-rays to check for broken bones, but otherwise he appeared to be fine, but shaken up and sore. Maybe slight concussion. Alice said she would be at the hospital soon.

Alice took a deep breath and then picked up her mobile phone, and called Paul to tell him what had happened.

"He was only here an hour ago," he said.

"It happened on the way home."

"Are you sure he is OK?"

"I haven't seen him yet, but the hospital says he is. I don't think they would say that if there was any doubt."

"Can I come up there with you?"

"Of course. There will probably be lots of waiting around, so I'll be glad of the company anyway. I'll pick you up in about fifteen minutes.

"Great. I'll see you then. I'll wait for you outside."

When Alice and Paul arrived at the hospital just over half an hour later, they spoke to a member of staff and was told that James was still being X-rayed. They were told he might be a while, but if they took a seat they would be informed when he came back. Alice thanked the nurse, and she and Paul got some foul-tasting coffee from a vending machine and sat down to wait.

2

By the time Simon Thompson got home, he was soaked in sweat and his mind was racing.

What had he done?

Why the hell had the stupid kid crossed the road without looking? The idiot was probably too engrossed in his mobile phone.

And why hadn't he just stopped the car after he'd hit him? That was all he had needed to do.

Panic.

That was the answer.

Simon Thompson had panicked – not so much about getting caught for hitting the kid, but about getting caught driving over the speed limit and while off his head.

What had he been thinking? It was obvious that Simon had not been thinking at all.

When he finally stepped out of the car, he used the torch on his mobile phone to check for damage to the vehicle. Something that would incriminate him. He couldn't see anything. Perhaps he hadn't hit the lad as hard as he thought. He was praying that was the case, not that he had been remotely religious until ten minute earlier. He would check the car again in the morning, just in case he had missed anything.

Simon turned the torch off and then let himself into his flat.

After taking off his jacket, he went through into the kitchen and poured himself a large, *very* large, brandy. He gulped it down and then poured another which he took through into the lounge and put it down beside the computer. The best thing to do was to let it boot up (which took a while these days) while he had a shower and calmed down, then he would check on Twitter for any news of the accident. Perhaps if he found out the boy wasn't killed, he might relax a bit.

The shower didn't calm him down, and neither did Twitter. There was no mention as yet of the accident. Simon tried to convince himself that was good news.

3

Jonathan and Andrew did a great deal of talking.

Jonathan chewed his way through the dried-up casserole, saying it was delicious in order to give

Andrew's ego a boost, although it was anything but. Still, he was just happy that Andrew had got out of his chair to do something.

And then the talking had begun. It started with Andrew asking if they were "back to normal." Jonathan could have just said that they were in order to have an easy life, but he knew that, long term, that wasn't the way forward. Things needed to be ironed out – and for good, not just to cover up cracks in the relationship temporarily. Changes needed to be made permanently if they were going to get through this as a couple.

"We've got things to sort out," Jonathan said.

"OK. What do you need me to do?" Andrew replied.

It wasn't the reply that Jonathan had expected, but he wasn't going to complain. Andrew was obviously currently in a place where he felt eager to please and put things right, although Jonathan was well aware that it might not last long.

"Well," he said, "you need to stop lying to me when you do something you know I won't like."

"What do you mean?"

"Like starting to drink again. You were doing it at work, Andrew. I can live with the fact you had started drinking, but not the fact you kept it from me, or that you allowed it to get in the way of doing your job properly. Those things are important. We worked through it together last time. We can do that again. But only if I know what's going on."

Jonathan went on to say that Andrew needed to be

more honest if he felt the depression issues were coming back. They both knew they could be managed if they were caught early enough. The current situation had only occurred because Andrew had tried to ignore what was happening, or, more accurately, hadn't been bothered to try to confront it.

Andrew agreed to everything, although Jonathan was well aware that it was never going to be that easy in practice. This was clearly a day when Andrew was feeling good, but tomorrow might be different. The irritability was likely to return.

The making-up sex was as good as it always was – and they'd had their fair share of practice at make-up sex over the course of their time together. Theirs had not been the smoothest of relationships, despite the fact they thought the world of each other.

They spent the next morning in bed, sometimes just lying there in silence, and at other times continuing their talk from the night before.

"I still think you should go to see a counsellor privately," Jonathan said. "This isn't going away overnight."

"It's a lot of money, Jon."

"And we can manage it. You know that as well as I do. We're not broke, and both at work. But if you don't get better, you might not be."

Andrew lay there in silence for a moment.

"OK," he said, eventually. "Besides, I don't think I have much choice, do I?"

"No, I don't think you do. Not if you want to go

back to work and prevent this from happening again."

"Alright. And what about us? Are we OK now?"

"We seemed fine last night, didn't we?"

"Better than ever, I'd say," Andrew said, grinning.

"And to think you were so innocent just a couple of years ago when we met. What on earth happened?"

"You," Andrew said. "You happened."

He pulled his boyfriend close and kissed him.

4

The hit-and-run made the local news the next morning.

Under normal circumstances, it might not have done, especially given James's minor injuries of concussion and a couple of cracked ribs, but this had been the third such incident in the city centre in less than a month. And, this time, there had been an eyewitness who was able to describe the make, model and colour of the car – all of which were familiar to Neil Moore.

Neil knew someone with a car that fit that exact description, and the owner of that car had visited his girlfriend the previous evening, something that Neil was less than impressed about.

He couldn't believe it when Claire had called to tell him that Jason had been to see her. He didn't think Jason would have the nerve, and he was annoyed with Mark for telling him that Claire was his girlfriend in the first place, as he wanted Jason to find out at just the right moment. He had told him to keep it quiet for the time being, but the truth was that Mark was still pissed off for being shouted at by Jason earlier in the week, and just couldn't help but tell him just to see the reaction.

Neil rang Claire again after he had seen the news.

"Tell me about Jason's visit again," he said.

Claire was confused.

"Why?" she asked. "I told you last night. He just came to apologise for how he treated me when we were going out. He said it had been playing on his mind, that's all."

"He didn't mention me?"

"Not really."

"Not really? What does that mean?"

"He just told me to say hi to you, that's all."

"I bet he did."

"What's going on, Neil? It's not like he did anything wrong."

"Of course, he didn't."

"I don't understand, Neil. What's wrong?"

"Nothing. Nothing is wrong. I promise."

When he ended the call, Neil pulled up the text message from Mark that he had received the evening before.

"Apparently Jason bashed his car on the way home from poker tonight. What an idiot," it read.

Neil knew that it wasn't Jason's car that had hit James, but the situation seemed too perfect for him not to take advantage of it. Jason's car fit the description, Jason knew the victim, and his car had damage to it.

What better way could there be for him to get his revenge? But he wouldn't jump into anything too quickly. He had to be sure he had thought everything through, so he wouldn't be caught out. He didn't want everything to blow up in his face and get himself in trouble.

5

Alice and Paul had finally got to see James about an hour after they arrived at the hospital. He seemed in surprisingly good spirits, although Alice wondered if shock would set in later. James said he was tired, but that was hardly surprising given everything that had happened.

They remained at the hospital for a few hours in order to make sure that James was really alright. By the early hours of the morning, all three of them were ready for sleep, and Alice and Paul went home, and James was transferred to a ward where he managed to get some rest. Paul decided to stay at James's house. He said it was to keep Alice company, but the truth was that he didn't want to be alone in the flat.

When Alice and Paul returned to the hospital that afternoon, James was being interviewed by a pair of police officers.

"And you remember nothing at all?" he was asked as they entered the room.

"Hey," James said to Paul and Alice, before turning his attention back to the police. "As I said, I don't remember anything," he went on. "I was putting my phone in my pocket as I stepped off the pavement, and the next thing I knew, I was in the ambulance. I didn't see the car, or, if I did, I don't remember. I couldn't tell you anything about it."

"It's OK. We have a description from an eyewitness. But if you do happen to remember anything else during the next few days, please let us know."

James nodded.

"I will," he said.

The police officers moved away, and Alice and Paul moved over to the bed. Paul sat down while Alice kissed her son on the forehead.

"How are you feeling, honey?" she asked him.

"I'm OK," James said. "A bit sore, but otherwise I'm fine. I've got a big bruise on my head, which hurts like hell. The nurse said I might be able to go home later today, but I've got to wait until the doctor comes around and see what he says."

"Are you sure you feel ready to come home?"

James smiled.

"Yes, Mum. I'm fine, honest. It could have been so much worse."

"You could have been killed."

"I'm well aware of that."

"Do you think it was deliberate?" Paul asked.

James shrugged his shoulders.

"I don't know. It's hard to tell. The police said there

have been two other hit-and-runs in the city centre in the last few weeks, but they don't know if this one is related to those. Now they've got a description of the car, they might be able to find out who did it, I guess. There's plenty of CCTV cameras in the area."

"Let's hope so," Alice said. "It wouldn't be so bad if they'd have stopped when they hit you."

"Somebody must have been there at the time and called for the ambulance, but I don't know who it was."

James was worried his mum was going to start crying again, and so changed the subject.

"Have you heard how Alfred's doing?" he asked. "He'll wonder what's happened if I don't go and see him this afternoon. I don't want him to think I've forgotten him."

"He won't do that. In fact, I'll go and see him now and let him know what has happened while you and Paul have some time together. I'll be back in a little while."

"Thanks, Mum. That would be great. Tell him I'll be in to see him as soon as I can."

Alice nodded, and then walked off and left James and Paul alone.

"What are the others like in this bay?" Paul whispered to James.

"They're OK," James replied. "Although none of them seem to stay long. Hopefully I won't either."

"We brought your phone charger," Paul said, digging it out of his pocket and handing it to James.

"Thanks."

"We couldn't bring your laptop because it's at uni."

"Yeah, I know."

"How long do you think you'll need to have off?"

"I don't know. I'll probably stay at home a week, I suppose. Just until I'm feeling a bit better."

"Do we need to let them know?"

"I'll send an email from my phone."

"I've arranged to stay at your place for a few days when you get out of here," Paul said. "Just to help your mum look after you."

"I'm not going to be stuck in bed when I get home. I can walk. They said I can have a shower if I stay in tonight."

"I'll help you have one when you get home."

James grinned.

"Won't be the first time!" he said.

"What did the police want?" Paul asked.

"Nothing much. They just wanted to know what I remembered from last night. I couldn't tell them anything, to be honest. It all happened so quick."

Oddly, despite everything that had happened, they had little to talk about, and their conversation was awkward and stilted, as hospital visits often are.

The doctor came while Paul was there, accompanied by a couple of medical students. They only spent a couple of minutes with James, and he was told that it would be best if he stayed another night in hospital, just to be on the safe side, but that he could definitely go home the next day.

"Really? I'd like to go home today if possible,"

James said. "I'd get more sleep at home than I would here."

The doctor didn't change his mind.

"It's not that bad, is it?" Paul said when the doctor had left. "It's only one more night."

"I know. It's just so bloody noisy. You just get off to sleep and someone's wheeled out of here, or someone else is wheeled in. I'd get more rest at home."

"Did you want us to bring anything? We could bring the books for your course that you brought back with you."

James thought about it for a moment. At least he could do some of the reading that he would have done for the first full week of lectures had he been at the university. But he doubted he would have been in the right frame of mind to concentrate on what he was doing. He wasn't even sure that he wanted to make the effort.

"No," he said. "It's fine. I don't think I'm in the mood, to be honest. They're not exactly light reading."

"Perhaps you can get some of it done while you're at home next week."

"Yeah, maybe."

But James wasn't sure that would happen.

His enthusiasm for university was currently virtually non-existent, and he was beginning to wonder if it would ever return. Paul, meanwhile, was hoping that it wouldn't.

6

Around noon, Neil left the house and walked to a phone box that was about a mile away. There was one closer to home that he could have used, but was worried that it might make it easier to trace the call back to him in some way. He made sure his face was covered as he went in.

He rang the local police station and told them he had some information on the hit-and-run from the night before, which he said he had witnessed. He gave them the same description of the car as the eyewitness on the local news, but he also told them the license plate number.

The person he spoke to on the telephone started pressing him for his name and address so that the officers in charge could speak to him, at which point Neil ended the call. He had said enough, and knew that Jason would now be implicated. He wasn't about to give away his identity.

As he walked away from the phone box, he felt pleased with himself for coming up with such a plan. He doubted Jason would be charged with anything as there would be no proof, but he liked the idea of him sweating it out for a few days.

Jason was out when the police arrived at his house.

On his return, he drove up the road towards his home, and wondered why there was a police car parked outside. At first, he panicked that something had happened to his mum or dad. From films and television shows that he had seen, that was often the reason why the police turned up unannounced. Or perhaps his dad's business dealings weren't as legal as they should have been and somebody had found out. That certainly wouldn't have surprised Jason. He had suspected something of that kind for months, but had never brought it up with his parents. He knew better than that. He was better off keeping quiet. If his dad got caught, that would be his problem, not Jason's.

He parked the car, got out, and then walked inside the house. As soon as he entered the hallway, he could see his dad and two police officers seated around the dining table. The TV was on in the lounge, and he guessed his mum was in there watching it. Nobody had died, after all. So, what was going on?

"At last he comes home!" his dad said from the dining room, and clearly not in a good mood. "About bloody time."

It was suddenly clear to Jason that the police were waiting for *him*, although he had no idea why, as he hadn't done anything wrong. He walked over to the dining room doorway.

"What's going on?" he said.

"That's what I'd like to know," Peter Mitchell replied. "These police officers want to speak to you, but they won't tell me why."

"Your son is over eighteen, Mr. Mitchell," one of the police officers said to him, quite clearly not for the first time, and the impatience with him was beginning to show. "We cannot disclose that kind of information to you."

"What the hell have you gone and done this time?" Jason's dad continued.

"I haven't done anything," Jason replied, and unlike two years earlier when newspaper reporters gathered outside the Mitchell household to ask questions about the article printed that day, Jason was telling the truth.

"Where have you been this morning?" his dad asked him.

"Out."

"*Where*?"

"For Christ's sake! I bumped the car last night when I parked it, so I took it to the garage to see how much it would cost to put right."

"Typical. Were you drunk?"

"No, Dad. I wasn't drunk. I hadn't been drinking at all. I just misjudged it. I never drink when I drive. You know that."

Peter Mitchell did not look convinced, despite the fact that there was no obvious reason to disbelieve his son.

"Mr. Mitchell, we need to speak to your son alone," one of the police officers said.

Jason's dad muttered to himself and walked out of the room.

"You're a bloody embarrassment," he said to his son as he walked past him.

"Thanks, Dad."

Jason went into the dining room and shut the door, and wondered if his dad had been told about art college already.

"What's this about?" he asked.

"Why don't you sit down, Jason?"

Jason thought it was a little odd being offered a seat in his own house, but sat down anyway.

"Am I in trouble?"

"We just need to ask you some questions about your movements last night," one of the officers said.

Jason was well aware that his question had not been answered, and it didn't put him at ease.

"Why?" he asked.

"There was a hit-and-run last night in the city centre, and a description of a car matching yours was given by an eyewitness."

This seemed straightforward enough. Jason could just tell them his whereabouts from the night before, and this would be over. He knew nothing about the accident, and certainly hadn't been a part of it.

"I was playing poker last night with some friends," he said, not adding that they might not be friends for much longer.

"What time was this?"

"Seven o'clock."

"And what time did you leave?"

"About nine. I was the first to leave. I lost quickly, unfortunately."

"And people can verify this?"

"Yes, of course."

Jason gave the names and addresses of Madeline, Mark, and Rick.

"What did you do when you left the game? Did you come straight home?"

Jason was tempted to say yes, but realised that telling the truth was the best way forward. The police would have little interest in his private life and how he was trying to keep an ex-friend quiet.

"No," he said. "I went to see an old friend on the way home."

He gave them Claire's name and address.

"Were you long at Miss Bramwell's house?"

"No. About ten minutes. That's all."

"That seems short for a social visit."

"She was a friend a couple of years ago. A girlfriend. I just went to see her because of something I wanted to clear up with her."

The police officers looked at each other as if this was important in some way, and that they might want to question him on this further, but they moved on.

"So, you left Miss Bramwell's house at 9.30pm and came straight home?"

"Yes. And as you already heard, I bumped the car when I parked. You can look at it when you go out if you want. You'll see the garage door is slightly scratched where it happened. Just don't tell Dad about that. He'll do his nut, as you can probably imagine."

"You don't have a good relationship with your father?"

"Not really."

"Any specific reason?"

"Does this have anything to do with the hit-and-run?"

The policeman shook his head.

"No," he said. "Just curious."

"My dad wants me to do one thing with my life, and I want to do something else with it. The idea of his son studying art isn't something he likes the idea of."

"I understand. So, you were nowhere near the high street at around 10.15?"

"No, I was at home."

"Can anyone verify that?"

"I doubt it. Mum and Dad weren't in when I got home. A neighbour might have seen me, I guess. Me hitting the garage door might have made enough noise for someone to notice."

"And you can't explain how your car was identified by an eyewitness of the hit-and-run on the High Street at 10.15 last night?"

"There are many cars like mine."

"But not with your number plates."

Jason felt like he had been punched in the stomach. He didn't understand. He hadn't been near there all night, so how could his car have been identified?

"The witness gave you *my* car's number? That's

not possible. I wasn't there. There's enough traffic cameras around here, you should be able to see me come home if you look at them."

For the first time in the conversation, Jason was beginning to get worried. Something was wrong. Very wrong. Suddenly, he remembered something which might help.

"If you're thinking that the damage to my car wasn't done how I said it was, I can prove it – and prove that it was done before 10.15."

"That would be useful."

Jason pulled his phone out of his pocket and pulled up the message that he had sent to Madeline the previous evening.

"Look," he said. "I'm telling her about the damage to the car in this message. The time on it says 9:38."

The police officers looked at the phone message.

"What do you mean in this message by saying that everything is going to be sorted soon?"

Jason didn't want to go into details about what had been going on, but he felt he didn't have much choice.

"I've just started going out with Madeline, and someone from my past has been threatening to tell her what an arsehole I was at school. I'm trying to stop him. I think I managed that by seeing Claire last night."

"Someone from your past?"

"Yes."

"Do you know someone by the name of James Marsh?"

The question came out of nowhere, and it was the

second time in quick succession that Jason had been caught off-guard. He had no idea what James had to do with what he was answering questions about.

"I did. I went to school with him. I'm guessing you already know that, though."

"You bullied him. Is that correct?"

"Yes. It all came out when the head of the school was forced to resign just before I left."

"Is Mr. Marsh the person from your past threatening to talk to your girlfriend?"

"No. Why? I haven't seen or heard from him in a long time."

"He was the victim of the hit-and-run last night."

"Is he OK?" Jason asked, his concern genuine.

"Relatively minor injuries. Him being the victim and your car being identified is something of a coincidence, don't you think?"

"I doubt it is a coincidence at all," Jason replied.

"Oh?"

"It's clear someone is framing me."

"Is it the person who is threatening you?"

"I wouldn't know."

"Can you tell us who it is who is threatening you?"

"I would rather not do that at this stage. I feel it would make things worse."

"With regards to this matter?"

"No. With regards to my life after you realise you've made a mistake."

The police officers stayed for another ten minutes. Before they left, they said to Jason that they were sure there was a "reasonable explanation" for his car having been seen on the high street by an eyewitness, but they didn't seem particularly sincere – something reiterated by them telling Jason to let them know if he remembered anything else that might be important.

He took that to mean that he should contact them if he decided to stop lying. The problem was that he wasn't lying. He had no idea what was going on. The whole thing was a mystery to him, and one that scared him.

Jason went up to his bedroom after the police officers left. His dad burst into the room a few minutes later.

"What the hell have you done?" he said as he came into the room.

Jason stood up and walked towards him.

"You should knock, Dad."

His dad smacked him around the head. It was the first time Jason could remember him laying a finger on him. Normally his dad wouldn't care enough to even bother.

"Don't smart-talk me. I heard what that was about. You *hit* someone in the car? *On purpose?*"

Jason stared at his dad. He realised that the two of them didn't know each other at all.

"If that's what you think, Dad, then you haven't a clue who I am. Now, fuck off out of my room."

He literally pushed his dad out of the door, and then shut it and slid the bolt across that he had put on a couple of years earlier without his dad even realizing. It had come in useful in recent weeks.

Peter Mitchell hammered on the door.

"Unlock this now, Jason! This is *my* house!"

"Yeah, it is," Jason shouted back, "until Mum works out who you're sleeping with and then divorces you."

The hammering stopped, and Jason heard his dad walk away.

8

Alice Marsh followed the rabbit warren-like maze of corridors around the hospital to the main cafeteria, and bought herself a cup of tea and sat down.

She had promised that she would go and see Alfred and tell him what had happened, therefore giving James and Paul some time together. She knew her conversation with Alfred wouldn't take long, though, so she took the time to have a coffee on the way. She needed time to think, or, at least, to put her existing thoughts in order – and she thought that the boys wouldn't object to being able to spend longer with each other, either.

Alice was worried about her son. Not because he had been hit by a car, although that was bad enough, but his physical wounds would heal. Probably quickly. No, what had concerned her much more was how he had hugged her and sobbed when he had arrived home the day before. She hadn't seen him in that state since the bullying at school two years earlier, and she had no idea what she should be doing about it. After all, she knew full well that nothing like that was happening now.

It appeared that she wasn't the only one with the same concerns.

After twenty minutes or so, she walked to the cardiology ward to speak to Alfred. She found him sitting in the chair beside the bed, fully dressed, and looking surprisingly healthy. She wasn't sure if he would know who she was as they had only met a couple of times, but she needn't have worried.

"Alfred?" she said, as she approached the bed.

"Well, well. Mrs. Marsh!" he said, his face lighting up. "What brings you here to see an old fogey like me? Did James ask you to call?"

"Yes," Alice said. "Yes, he did. How are you?"

"Oh, I'm doing fine. They say I'll be alright as long as I behave myself. As if I plan to start doing that at my age!"

He winked at her, and she smiled for probably the first time that day.

"Well, sit down, my dear. Sit down."

Alice sat down on the edge of the bed.

"Has James gone back to university already?" Alfred asked.

Alice shook her head, not quite sure how to break the news of the accident to Alfred without worrying him.

"No, he won't be going back for a week or so now. There was an accident, Alfred. James was hit by a car on

218

the way home from Paul's last night."

Alfred's face drained of colour.

"Is he alright?" he asked.

"Yes, he'll be fine. They say he has a couple of cracked ribs, and he had concussion. But he will mend soon enough. They are keeping him in for a couple of days, so he asked me to come and tell you why he isn't visiting you today."

Alfred nodded his head slowly.

"I understand," he said. "Thank you for letting me know. What happened?"

"He stepped off the curb to cross the road, wasn't totally paying attention to what he was doing from what I can understand, and a speeding car hit him. They didn't stop. The nurses are saying he was very lucky not to have been seriously injured. Or worse."

Alfred nodded again.

"Ah, yes," he said. "I heard about it on the wireless. I had no idea it was Jim who was hit, of course. That's terrible. The poor lad. He doesn't have much luck, does he? They didn't catch the driver, I suppose?"

"No, not as far as I am aware."

"The news said there had been two others like it over the last few weeks. I don't think they got off as lightly, from what they were saying. You sure he's alright?"

Alice reassured him that James was fine.

"I feel so responsible," Alfred said. "If it wasn't for me having this stupid heart attack, he would still be at the university."

"Nonsense," Alice responded. "You can't blame yourself. Anyway, he's going to be OK, that's the main thing."

"Physically, at least," Alfred said. "But Master James isn't happy, is he?" he said after a few seconds.

Alice sighed.

"No. And I'm not quite sure what any of us can do about it."

"Do you know what the issue is? He hasn't told me everything, I don't think."

"Not completely. It is all linked to school, of course. It always is, even after all this time. I think it has all caught up with him. These things do, I suppose."

Alfred nodded in agreement.

"Yes," he said. "Yes, they do. And most often it is at the time when we least expect it. It's like grieving, I suppose. One day you're fine, and the next you're back where you started. I know that from my wife. One day I'm as right as rain, and the next I'm crying like a baby because a song she liked comes on the wireless. And it has been years now. I miss her so much, Mrs. Marsh. If she was still around, I'd have let the shop go by now. But I don't want to grieve for that, too. She'd have liked Jim, you know? She would have spoiled him rotten."

He smiled a sad smile and changed the subject.

That evening, Jason sat in the pub with Madeline. He told her everything that had happened over the past twenty-four hours, including the visit to Claire. At this point, the best thing he could do was tell the truth, even if painted him in a bad light

"Something doesn't seem right," Madeline said.

Jason nodded in agreement.

"It's been bothering me all day," he said. "But I haven't been able to put my finger on it."

"Coincidences," Madeline said, defiantly. "Coincidences never seem right. You bash your car. Half an hour later, someone you bullied at school is knocked over, and an eyewitness then identifies your car with your number plates. And yet you weren't there. Something doesn't add up."

"You're telling me."

"And you know what I think? I think the police don't believe the eyewitness either. If they did, they would have arrested you. And if someone saw your car last night when the accident happened, they would have given your number plates to the police there and then, and the police wouldn't have waited till this afternoon to come and see you. This is someone who has come forward *after* hearing the description of the car on the news.

Jason realised Madeline was right.

"I may be barking up the wrong tree, but I think I know who this supposed eyewitness might be," Jason said.

"Me, too," Madeline replied. "But the big question is, what are you going to do about it? You can't be sure that he has set you up. What if we're wrong?"

Jason thought for a moment.

"I'm going to wait," he said.

When he got home that night, Jason sat on the bed and started drawing.

He drew a picture of Neil Moore how he was on the last day of school, taped to the lamp post and covered in food - the event that caused all of Jason's current troubles.

It seemed so long ago now. So much had happened during the past two years, and most it surprisingly positive. Jason wasn't going to let someone with a grudge undo his hard work.

He stared at the picture when it was finished, and then tore it into pieces and threw it in the bin.

CHAPTER ELEVEN

1

The next morning, James was told by the doctor that he could leave hospital providing he promised to take things easy for a few days. He was eager to go home, and didn't take much persuading, and so promised he would, making arrangements for his mum to pick him up around noon. James had no intention of staying in the hospital any longer than he needed to, not least because he wanted his own bed and some home-cooked food.

With an hour to kill, James walked down to Alfred's ward, something which took a little longer than expected as his ribs seemed to hurt with each step that he took. He realised he was going to have no choice but to take it easy while they healed. Visiting hours weren't due to start for a while, but James explained the situation to one of the nurses and she allowed him to see his friend as long as he agreed not to stay too long.

Alfred was dressed and sitting in the chair beside the bed, just as he had been the day before, but he looked more tired than he had when James had seen him previously. Even so, he smiled broadly when James walked up to him.

"So," Alfred said, "you just had to copy me and get everyone worried about you, did you?"

"Don't go there, Alfred," James said. "This weekend has been a nightmare, hasn't it?"

"Yes, I'll agree with you on that. And yet we have both come through it."

James looked at Alfred, and thought that he had aged almost overnight.

"How are you, Alfred? You look tired."

"Oh, that's right. Make me feel better, why don't you? That's all I need!"

"Sorry."

"Don't you worry yourself. All I need is a good meal or two and a few nights in my own bed, and I'll be as good as new. These beds are so bloody hard."

"You should try the ones at uni."

"I've tried uni ones a few times myself. Long time ago, of course!" Alfred said with a wink.

"Too much info, Alfred!" James said, somewhat louder that he had intended.

"It is so damned noisy in here at night, too," Alfred went on. "It's almost as if they don't *want* us to sleep!"

"Have your family been to see you?" James asked. Alfred sighed.

"No, Jim-lad. I don't have a family that care enough

to come and visit me in hospital. I'm not even sure they know I'm in here. How would they find out? Perhaps they might if I was rich and they thought I was about to pop my clogs. But not as things stand. I'm neither rich *or* about to die just yet. No, Jim. *You're* my family these days. You know that."

James felt bad for his friend. He suddenly realised how lucky he was to have his mum, his sister, and Paul. And Adam had been in contact via Facebook as well. He wondered who Adam was spending time with at university while James wasn't there.

"When can you go home? Have they told you yet?" James asked.

"Tomorrow," Alfred said. "They always say tomorrow. It's like that song from *Annie*: 'It's always a bloody day away!' They want to do more tests today, apparently. So, perhaps I can go home if they're OK. I feel fine. Just tired. I need to recharge my batteries."

"I know what you mean," James said. "Except that mine shouldn't be run down."

"Oh, I don't know. You've had a big change to deal with during the last week or so, Master James. Going to university and settling in. It's not as easy as some people make out. Moving away is an upheaval. You're not used to it. "

"But that's the point. I haven't settled in. I'm not even sure I'm going to."

"What's the problem?"

Alfred had asked a question that James didn't know the answer to. He didn't know what the problem was.

He had been working towards going to university for the previous two years. That had been the whole point of A-levels. University had always been what he was aiming for. And now that he was there, he didn't know if it was what he wanted.

"It just doesn't feel right, Alfred," he said. "Not for me."

Alfred remained silent while James got his thoughts together.

"We're treated like machines," James said. "As if we're all the same. Clones of each other. If we do well at GCSEs, then we're steered towards A-Levels. We're not forced into it, but you almost have to make an effort to opt out of them. And if it looks like we're doing well at A-Levels, then it's expected that we are going to university. We're not forced, but it's expected. It's like we're on a conveyer belt, and if we don't want to reach the end, we have to make the effort to jump off. Do you know what I mean?"

"But your mum expects nothing of you. Neither does Paul. Or me."

"No. But The System does. And we don't realise it until it's too late."

James had spent the evening before chatting to a mature student from the Politics Society at university on Facebook Messenger. He had only started university in his late thirties.

"I went when I was eighteen," the man had said. "But it wasn't the right time for me, and I quit after a few months. Now it *is* the right time, but I'm nearly forty."

Something about what the man had told him had struck a chord with James. It made sense to him. He understood what he was talking about.

"Why is it that it is expected that we are all able to leave home and go to university at eighteen or nineteen?" James said to Alfred. "Or that we all should do our A-levels at a certain time in our lives. Or even retire. It's not like we all grow up at the same time, or become mature in other ways at the same time. We don't all have our first drink at the same age. Or first have sex. Or have our first kiss. Or…" James fumbled around for another example. "Am I talking bollocks?" he said, finally.

Alfred smiled.

"No, James. You're working through your feelings and thoughts, and that is perfectly normal and healthy. And eventually, you'll suddenly realise what is right for *you*. That might mean going back to university next week. Or next year. Or in ten years. Or maybe never. You don't *have* to go. Nobody will think any less of you if you don't. You're right, everyone is different, but it's also something you need to talk to your mum about. And Paul. See what they have to say."

James said that he would.

"And James," Alfred went on. "Never forget that I am so proud of you. Listening to you talking like that. Thinking for yourself. You're quite the young man I always knew you would be."

"Thanks, Alfred," James said, and then told him that

he had to go, but would visit him the next day, whether he was back at home or still in hospital.

Before he left, James bent down and kissed the old man on the forehead. It was something he had never done before.

2

Jonathan didn't have to go to the office very often on a Sunday, but this week was an exception, although he knew he would be finished by around midday and so arranged to meet Andrew for a carvery lunch, thinking it would do him good to get out of the house now that he seemed to be feeling a bit better.

Andrew didn't feel as well or as energetic as he had the day before. He seemed tired, and his mind was more than a little foggy, but he seemed to take it in his stride rather than seeing it a setback of any significance, although it had taken him longer to shower and get ready than usual.

"I'm not going to get better all at once," he said to Jonathan as they sat eating their dinner. "I can't expect miracles."

Both of them had opted for the roast beef, although Andrew, knowing his appetite wasn't back to normal, opted for a child's portion and then wished he'd gone for an adult's as he started to tuck in.

"That's true," Jonathan said. "And I think it's a good

thing that you know that. That in itself is probably a big step forward."

Andrew agreed, and sipped at the glass of water in front of him.

"We'll get there. I know that now," he said

"Well, your appetite is back, I see."

"Seems like it. Perhaps I'll go back for seconds."

Jonathan put down his knife and fork a moment.

"I heard something bizarre at work today," he said.

"Yeah?"

"Did you hear about the hit-and-run on the High Street on Friday night?"

Andrew nodded.

"Yeah. It's been on the local news."

"The person who got hit was James Marsh."

Andrew looked at Jonathan with disbelief.

"Really? Is he OK?"

"Yeah. From what we've heard from 'sources,' he was in hospital for a day or two, but out now."

"I'm surprised he's still in town. The last time I bumped into him, he said he was going to university. Semester started last week or the week before."

"Perhaps he changed his mind. He could have deferred or something."

"Maybe, but he seemed quite excited about it."

"But there's more to the story. It's not official, but the suspect is Jason Mitchell."

This time it was Andrew's turn to put down his knife and fork.

"You're joking, right? Who told you that?"

"You know I can't tell you that. And we wouldn't print it unless an arrest is made anyway. We can at least have some scruples as a local paper. But that's not the point. It's weird, isn't it?"

"It's not weird, Jon. It's wrong. Jason wouldn't do that."

"You seem very sure."

"I *am* sure. He's done lots of horrible things, but he wouldn't do that."

"They have his number plates from an eyewitness."

"*Really?*"

"I understand there is some doubt over the eyewitness, though. It was an anonymous tip."

"The police can't use it, then, can they?"

"I doubt it. Not unless they can get something else to back it up."

"Jason has lots of enemies, I should imagine, even from his own crew. And I'm sure they would be quite happy to set him up for something he didn't do – or try to set him up, at least. I understand why they would want payback."

Andrew thought for a moment or two.

"You know, that's where it went wrong," he went on. "The one thing that I regret about what happened two years ago. We were meant to bring down The Head, not destroy Jason."

"One was always going effect the other."

"Yes, but we didn't think it through enough."

"The wonders of hindsight. You couldn't have foreseen that Jason was going to jump in the river to try to save someone he was bullying, and therefore make the headlines anyway. His name would probably have never come out if he hadn't done that. That's what brought him into it. Wrong place and wrong time. It was inevitable that people would join the dots. It wasn't us who made his name public. The name of the bully wasn't given."

"Even so. I feel bad for him. His dad was an arsehole, and The Head did everything he could to stop Jason getting the punishment he deserved. Had he got it, he might not have carried on."

"You don't know that."

"No. But Jason could have been helped, too. He's had to live with the reputation he ended up with. That can't have been easy."

"It's a problem of his own making, Andrew."

"Yes. And he was an exasperating, vicious little bastard. But he was sixteen, and had plenty of time to change if given the right guidance and opportunities – which he wasn't given at home or at school from what I saw. Through all the years I've taught, I've never known a single kid who was all good or all bad. I'm sure he was no different. We can't give up on people when they're still teenagers. Perhaps that is a story for you one day, Jonathan. It's not just the victims who have problems later in life, but the bullies too."

3

Jason had been sitting in his car across the street from James's house for over an hour when he saw the family car pull up outside and James, his mum and Paul got out. Jason watched them go into the house and wondered how long he should wait until he disturbed them.

He had no real idea of what he was doing there or what he planned to say to James if and when he got to speak to him. He realised that James might not have any clue that Jason was under suspicion for the hit-and-run, but, either way, he had to make it clear to him, no matter what he might hear to the contrary, that he had nothing to do with what had happened to him. He had no control over anything else, even over whether he would be arrested or not, although he didn't think he would be, but he would at least make sure that James knew the truth.

The situation was horrible. James had got hurt, Jason had been implicated, the real driver was still out there, and Badger's actions almost certainly meant that Claire would suffer at the hands of two boyfriends in succession – because the truth would eventually come out, and she would find out what Badger had done. Jason was sure of that. He had to be. He couldn't allow himself to think otherwise.

Meanwhile, that morning, Jason's mum and dad had had the biggest row of their marriage. Despite it being a relatively loveless affair at the best of times, there was rarely enough interest from either party for an argument to erupt. But when Jason's mum found out that her son had been hit by her husband, that all changed.

Jason sat up in his room as World War Three started in the lounge, and had no interest in going downstairs either to stop it or take part. He was quite content to hear them shout and scream at each other. It was what they deserved. At least one ornament (hopefully an expensive one) got thrown towards Peter Mitchell, and ended up smashing against the wall behind him. Jason also heard his mum say that he had enrolled at the college whether they liked it or not, and that she wasn't sure why they should be so against it.

Jason wondered if perhaps something good would come out of the argument, after all, although he doubted that his dad would change his mind about Jason's plans. He wondered what would happen if his parents found out how he was currently raising the fees.

While he was waiting in the car, Jason got a text message from Madeline asking if he was OK and whether there was any further news. He wrote back to say he was fine, and that there wasn't. Jason was at least pretty sure now that Madeline was on his side and would stay by him, no matter what. That was something to be thankful for.

Just after receiving the text, the front door to James's house opened and James walked slowly down the path and crossed the road towards Jason's car. At first, Jason panicked that he had been spotted, and thought he should start the car and drive away. Instead, he took a deep breath and got out of the car. James walked up to him.

"I've no idea why you're here, Jason," he said, "but I'm guessing you want to speak to me or Paul."

"Yeah, sorry," Jason said. "I saw you come home, and I was just giving you a bit of time before I disturbed you."

"I think seeing you staring at the house is disturbing enough."

"Sorry," Jason said again. "I heard you'd been in hospital."

"Word gets around quickly."

Jason forced a smile.

"Why don't you come in?" James asked.

"Thanks."

James and Jason crossed the road, and went inside.

4

It wasn't Simon Thompson's conscience that resulted in him walking into the police station that afternoon, but his fear.

Had the hit-and-run not been discussed in the media in relation to the two previous incidents, then he probably would never have turned himself in. Had that been the case, Jason's future might have turned out quite differently. However, Simon knew there was a chance that, if he was somehow caught or his car identified, he wouldn't be charged with just one of the accidents, but all three of them. And he was only guilty of one. He didn't want to pay the price for things he hadn't done, and at least the news report had stated that the injuries from Friday's incident were minor.

Thompson had been high two nights earlier when he had driven down the high street at nearly double the speed limit and hit the teenager who had stepped off the pavement in front of him. If he hadn't been high, he would have stopped – or so he kept telling himself, but he couldn't have risked getting arrested in that state.

But the guilt and the fear of being caught gnawed away at him for the next forty-eight hours, and at 2pm he went to the police station to confess to what he had done. He couldn't remember ever having been in a police station before – something that suddenly struck him as strange as he walked over to the front desk and told the officer why he was there.

5

When James returned to the house with Jason, Alice Marsh got the boys some drinks and then left the living room and made herself busy elsewhere. She had no idea why Jason had come to see James. She knew he had already apologised for the distress he had caused her son, but she doubted that he was there so that he could express his sympathy for the accident. Either way, she knew that James, Paul and Jason would want to be left alone to talk, no matter how curious she was to find out why what was going on. She was sure she would be told the details later.

"I heard about your accident," Jason said. "I hope you're OK."

"I'll be fine," James replied. "Just a couple of cracked ribs. Nothing to worry about really. I was lucky."

"I guess you were."

None of them wanted to be in the room at that moment. The boys were not remotely comfortable in each other's company, despite two years having passed.

"This is awkward, isn't it?" Jason said.

"Yeah," James said, "so why don't you tell us why you're here? Or lurking across the street."

Jason took a deep breath.

"I had to come here because I need you to realise that, whatever you might hear, it wasn't me."

"What wasn't you?" Paul asked.

"It wasn't me that hit James in the car."

James was confused.

"I never thought it was you," he said. "Why would I think that? What's going on?"

"The police think it's me. Someone told them they saw my car. Someone said that it was my car that hit you. But I was nowhere near the high street on Friday night. I was at home when it happened."

"Perhaps they were confused. It was probably just a similar car."

"They gave my number plates. *My* number plates. But it wasn't me. I was at home by the time of the accident. I need you to believe me."

"I believe you," James said. "I promise. But how could that happen? And if they have an eyewitness that gave your number plates, how come you haven't been arrested?"

Jason shrugged his shoulders.

"I don't know," he said. "Perhaps the police realise something doesn't ring true. I don't know."

"Maybe," Paul said, although he was considerably less believing of Jason than James was, and his demeanour didn't hide it. He didn't understand why Jason was there if he hadn't been behind the wheel.

"Someone has set you up?" James said.

"I think so."

"Who is it? Do you know?"

"Maybe. But not for certain."

"But the police smell a rat?" James said.

"No," Jason replied, before adding: "Not a rat. A *Badger.*"

James and Paul looked at each other, not quite sure if they were understanding Jason correctly.

"You're saying *Badger* hit James?" Paul asked. "Was he driving your car?"

"No, I know he didn't hit James. He was playing poker at the time."

"Badger plays poker?"

"He does lots of thinks he didn't used to. You'd be surprised. But I think he gave the police my number plates."

"Why would he do that?"

"It's a long story. I hadn't seen him since school until a week ago. He turned up at a poker game I was having with some friends. He saw that I was happy with my new girlfriend, Madeline, and he tasted blood. He's already threatened to tell her what I was like at school – although I've told her everything now so that he can't gain anything by doing that. My guess is that the stars aligned for him on Friday. I pranged my car when I was parking that night, and the local news said that a car like mine was seen at the accident. Badger saw an opening. A chance. And so I reckon he came forward with my registration number."

"Do you know this for sure?" James asked.

Jason shook his head.

"No," he said. "It just fits. It's the *only* thing that fits. He wants to get back at me for treating him badly at school. He's even going out with Claire, would you believe?"

"Poor Claire," Paul said.

"Too right. First me, then him. What's she done to deserve that?"

At that moment, Jason's phone started to ring. He took it out of his pocket and looked at the screen.

"I don't recognize the number. I'd better take it," he said, and went out into the hallway.

He returned two minutes later, looking somewhat relieved.

"That was the police," he said. "They have arrested

the person responsible for the accident. And they're sorry for any inconvenience, blah blah blah."

"That's great," James said to him. "Great for you and great for me to know they've got the guy."

"What are you going to do about Badger?" Paul asked.

"I'm going to give him a visit."

"Don't do anything you regret, Jason," James said. "You've just dodged a bullet. Don't end up shooting yourself in the foot."

Jason nodded, thanked them for their time, said his goodbyes and then left. He got in his car and drove to Badger's flat – Jason no longer even tried to think of him as "Neil." He would forever be known by the nickname he apparently hated so much.

6

Jason was convinced that he had done as good a job as possible of trying to right his past wrongs, and to move forward with his life, but dealing with Badger meant that, just for a few minutes, he was willing to become the vindictive bully that he had been over two years earlier.

He was angry, and he wasn't about to let Badger get away with what he had done. He was thankful that no long-lasting damage had occurred, and that Badger's attempt to set him up had failed, but now that he had been cleared it was time to make sure that Badger never did anything remotely similar to him, or anyone else, again. And no matter how nasty things got, Badger wasn't going to call the police on Jason – to do so would give the game away as to who had given the false information.

"Was it you?" Jason asked him when Badger was stupid enough to open the front door of his flat.

"Was what me?"

Jason pushed him.

"You set me up, you little shit."

"I don't know what you're talking about."

"You're a crap liar, Badger. You always were."

"What are you doing here?" Badger asked him. "You'd better go, or I'll…"

"What? Call the police? I thought you had already done that."

Jason pushed Badger out of the way and then barged into the flat. He opened the door to each room, checking that Badger's flatmates were not home, and then marched through into the kitchen, and pulled open all of the drawers until he found what he was looking for.

"What the hell are you doing?" Badger asked him.

Jason didn't reply, but he found what he was looking for.

Armed with the biggest knife he could find in Badger's kitchen, he went through to the lounge. He looked around, trying to find the best outlet for his anger. Badger was worried he was going to turn the knife on him, and yelled at him to stop, that he was sorry. Jason took no notice and started to slash away at the sofa with the knife. Each time Badger approached him to try to pull him away, Jason just thrust the knife in his direction as a warning to keep his distance. Badger could do nothing as he watched the sofa become a wreck of exposed foam and shredded material. He thought about calling the police, but knew he couldn't do that.

Next on Jason's list was the TV. He knocked it to the floor and then jumped and stamped on it until the screen was smashed beyond repair. He did the same with the laptop that was on the coffee table, literally throwing it across the room, before kicking over the table itself.

Finally, he threw down the knife, and turned his attention to Badger himself. He grabbed him by his shirt and pushed him up against the wall.

"Please don't," Badger whimpered, but Jason had no intention of stopping now.

"Is that all you're going to say?" Jason screamed at him. "How long have you known me? You think whimpering is going to stop me?"

His old friend and stooge became a punching bag for the longest thirty seconds of his life. Badger screamed as much through fear as pain as his nose crunched under Jason's fist and droplets of blood splattered over the wall. Eventually, Jason threw him to the floor and watched as Badger pleaded with him for a few seconds, while Jason moved his foot as if about to start kicking him.

"If you tell Claire or your flatmates I had anything to do with this, I'll be back to finish the job," he said to Badger. "Do you understand?"

Badger nodded.

"I won't tell anyone."

"There's a good boy," Jason said as he walked out of the flat.

With the exception of Badger's face, everything Jason had taken his rage out on had belonged to the other occupants of the flat. They had no insurance. Jason hadn't stopped to contemplate such things. To him, it was Badger's flat that had been destroyed and that was all that mattered, and he hadn't felt this good in two and a half years.

CHAPTER TWELVE

1

Alfred was the first to know. Had he not been, things might have turned out differently.

He was allowed to go home from hospital the day after James and, as promised, James visited him at home each day. For the first couple of days, he timed his visit with lunch so that Alfred could eat without having to prepare the meal himself. It was one way of making sure that he rested for at least some of the day. At the same time, it gave James something to do to take his mind off his own issues.

Paul and James's mum had continually questioned James about how he was and when he was planning to go back to university. Alfred never did, and James silently thanked him for it. The old man realised that James needed space to try and work out what he wanted to do. James knew that he wasn't being pressured at home as such, but Alfred barely mentioned the subject at all. It was sometimes like he could read James's mind and know what he wanted or needed.

On Alfred's third day at home, James said:

"I'm going back to university on Monday."

Alfred sipped at the cup of tea that James had made for him.

"You made up your mind, then?"

"Yes," James said. "I had to decide at some point. I couldn't keep putting it off. The longer I took, the more behind I would get on any work. But I'm going back there on Monday. I'm going to pack my belongings, take the room key to the office, and then come back home."

Alfred put the cup back in the saucer.

"You're not going to stay?"

James shook his head.

"No. I wrote them an email last night. They have offered to defer my entry for a year, and I may well take them up on that in case I change my mind. But I doubt I will go back."

"Are you sure this is really what you want to do?" Alfred asked.

"You think I should do something different?"

"No. Not at all. I'm just making sure that is what you want to do and that you haven't been influenced by anyone else. It has to be *your* choice."

James nodded.

"It is, Alfred," he said. "University isn't right for me. Not yet, anyway. I know that now. This isn't the right time."

"Have you told your mum and Paul yet?"

"No. Not yet. I wanted you to be the first to know. I'm going to do it when I get home this afternoon."

"Do it tomorrow," Alfred said.

"Tomorrow? Why tomorrow?"

"Just trust me. Tomorrow will be the right day to do it."

James was bemused by Alfred's keenness for him to put off talking to his mum and Paul for twenty-four hours, but agreed to it nonetheless. He thought he was perhaps being told to sleep on it just once more to make sure. What he didn't know was that Alfred had been coming to some decisions too, and he needed a few more hours to make the necessary telephone call to try and convince others that they were the right ones and that they would work.

Just before James left Alfred, he broached the subject that had been playing on his mind all morning.

"Alfred, I know you were talking about closing the shop for good. But if you keep it open…"

Alfred smiled at him.

"You don't need to worry about that," he said. "Believe me."

2

Jason had been tempted to go to see Claire again in order to tell her about what had been happening with Badger, but he decided against it, not least because she probably would have already found out about the beating that Badger had received from him. If Badger had told her some other story about he got injured, then Jason going to see her would make her figure out the truth for herself anyway. The less people who knew the truth, the better. Besides, she would never believe what Jason had to say, and he couldn't blame her for that.

Jason thought he would feel guilty for trashing Badger's flat and beating him up, but he didn't. In fact, he was strangely numb about it. Perhaps that was because he had used it as an outlet for his rage and had got it out of his system. He tried to tell himself that, but he also wondered if he had really left his old ways behind him as much as he thought he had. Perhaps those kinds of instincts would always hide somewhere within him, occasionally rising to the surface at certain times. Either way, there was nothing he could do about what he had done now. Badger was never getting an apology, and what was done was done.

He had briefly seen Rick and Mark at college, and neither of them had mentioned what happened to Badger, but they didn't ask Jason if he was planning to play poker at the end of the week either. It didn't come as a surprise. Madeline was subdued too, and Jason suspected that she had found out about what he had done and was trying to digest it, and maybe work out whether she wanted to be going out with someone capable of such things. She didn't break up with him, however, and they made arrangements to see each other a couple of nights later.

Three days after the beating of Badger, Jason returned home from college to find his mother waiting for him. As he entered the house, she called him through into the lounge and told him somberly to sit down. Jason did as he was told, realizing that something was up, and half expecting to be told that divorce proceedings were underway.

"You've had a difficult week," his mum said, "and I don't think your father and I were there to help you, or to guide you, in the way that we should have been."

Jason said nothing. He had no idea where this was going. If it was working up to an apology, then it would be the first one he could ever remember getting from either of his parents.

"When the police came at the weekend, your father assumed that you were guilty of causing that accident, and he was wrong to do so. He was even more wrong to hit you. I never allowed him to do that when you were a baby, and I'm certainly not going to allow that to happen now."

Jason realised that, despite edging closer to it, an apology still wasn't forthcoming, even if it was his father who should have given it and not his mother.

"Tomorrow when you go to the bank," his mother went on, "you will see that there has been a credit of five thousand pounds. That is to pay your fees for college this year, as well as any materials you need to buy, and some money for day to day expenses. Your father took a lot of persuading, but he agreed in the end. I can't promise the same for next year. If you need any extra money for disposable income, you will have to get a job and earn it. It will not come from us. Is that understood?"

Jason nodded his head solemnly.

"Yes," he said. "I understand. Thank you."

"Good. I hope you get out of these arts courses whatever you are hoping for. Or, at least, you get it out of your system. It's not what we would have wanted for you, but we can't choose the direction of your life forever, and perhaps we never did make a very good job of it. You were nineteen last month, and now it's time for you to do what you think is best. I just hope this isn't a fad and that you follow it through rather than just waste another year."

There was an awkward silence, and then Jason thanked his mum again and got up to leave. As he reached the door, his mum stopped him.

"Jason," she said. "It has been noticed how you have done your best to move forward since your accident, even if we don't talk about, or acknowledge, it. It is good that you are less wayward now."

Jason forced a smile and went up to his bedroom.

Perhaps the comments from his mother were more than he should or could have expected. They were as near as he would get to an apology, and there was even an acknowledgment that Jason had tried hard to change his ways. Little did his mother know about what he had done to Badger just three days earlier.

All Jason really cared about, though, was the

money. He now had the funds to pay for his courses, and wouldn't have to worry about that again for another year. Even if the regular handouts from his parents stopped as a result of the payment of the fees, Jason could easily manage if he carried on performing on webcam. Providing Madeline didn't find out, that probably wouldn't bother him. Or perhaps he could tell her, and she might join him in front of the camera occasionally, although he doubted that.

Even so, things had changed. He thought that the poker nights were almost certainly a thing of the past, and college was going to be a lonelier place without the friendship of Rick and Mark. But he would manage.

He had Madeline now.

3

That night, James and Paul talked in hush tones for a while in their bedroom and then had celebratory sex. No-one else knew yet just *what* they were celebrating, and the sex itself was rather restrained due to James's ribs. But it happened, nonetheless.

The next morning, James and Paul lay in bed when they heard the doorbell ring. They assumed it was the postman with something too big to fit through the letterbox, but a minute or so later, Alice Marsh called up to James to tell him that he had a visitor.

James and Paul put on their dressing gowns and

went downstairs. They went into the lounge and saw Alfred sitting on the sofa alongside James's mum.

"Good morning, Master James," Alfred said. "I thought I would come and see *you* for a change. Sorry if I'm a bit early for you."

James and Paul sat down.

"I said I'd come and see you later," James said, confused. "You didn't have to come here."

James began to wonder what was going on. Something was not right.

"What are you doing here?" he asked.

"Well, perhaps I have come to see your beautiful mother."

Alice Marsh playfully swiped at him.

"Flirt!" she said, laughing.

"Me?" Alfred said. "I'm innocent!"

Suddenly, the atmosphere got more serious.

"Alfred rang me yesterday to tell me you've decided not to go back to university," Alice said.

"Alfred!" James said, disappointed that his friend had told her.

"Hang on a minute," Alice Marsh said. "He did it for the right reasons."

"I'm not going to change my mind."

"And nobody is going to try to make you. But Alfred had something that he wanted to talk to me about. Ask my permission about, actually."

James was confused.

"I don't understand. Ask your permission about what?"

Alfred leaned forward.

"Jim. You asked me a few days ago if my family had been to see me in hospital. And I said no, and that you were my family. Do you remember?"

James nodded.

"OK. Well, I spoke to your mum because I had a proposal for you, but I wanted her opinion first. You worked at the shop for two years and you enjoyed it, I think?"

"Of course I did, Alfred. You know that."

"The problem is that I can't keep the shop going on forever, Jim. This last week has shown that. I'm too old and too tired to be bothered with going down and opening up every day. And the place looks old and tired, too. It needs a new lease of life if it's going to work, especially in this day and age. And I don't have that."

James didn't know where this was going.

"So, you're going to sell it?"

Alfred turned to look at Alice, as if asking for permission to carry on. She nodded her head and smiled.

"No, I'm not going to sell it. What I would like is for you to come and work there full-time for the next six months. I'll be there too, for much of the time. When I can. But I would be guiding you, showing you how things work beyond working the till and making cups of tea. I want you to come up with some ideas that you'd like to try. You've told me for ages that much of the stock should be listed online and that it would create more of a turnover. Well, you can try that. And play around with the window displays, and things like that. And I would teach you things like the book-keeping and filling in tax returns. The exciting side of shop-keeping!" Alfred grinned and winked at James. "In other words, you would be running the shop, and I would just be guiding you."

James was getting more confused. What Alfred was saying didn't quite make sense.

"So you're going to employ me for six months? But then what?"

"Then, if it's what you want, and you feel you can cope with the running of it, the shop is yours."

James looked at Alfred, dumbfounded.

"I don't understand. It's your shop Alfred. You can't just say it's mine."

"You're my *family*, Jim. It is in my will that it would be left to you anyway. If you decide to go back to university next year or some other time in the future then we can sort something out. That would always come first. Perhaps you could employ Paul to run it for you while you're gone. But we're talking about *now*, not some time in the future."

"Alfred wanted to run the idea by me first. You don't have to say yes, James," Alice said. "It's an offer, that's all. If you decide you don't want to…"

"Of course I want to!"

"Listen," his mother said, trying to calm him down. "If you want to think about it, or decide you don't want to when it's time to take over in six months, then no-one is going to hold that against you. Do you understand that?"

James said that he did, and then got up and hugged Alfred.

"I love you," he said. "Thank you."

"I love you, too," Alfred replied. "We'll give it a couple of weeks for us to both get a bit healthier and then we can get started. But I warn you, the paperwork is as boring as hell."

"It'll be fine. I just feel bad that you're losing your shop."

"I'm not losing it, Jim. I'm finding the right person to give it the best shot of staying afloat. And you're going to have to make some changes for that to happen. It doesn't make the money it used to. But you've got six months to see what you can come up with in that regard. You can do whatever you do online and see if it works."

"I will. We'll make it work."

"Then that's settled."

James couldn't believe what had happened, although his brain was buzzing with both ideas for the shop and worries that it wouldn't work out for one reason or another. Alfred had been honest in the past about how poorly the shop was doing, and James knew that it would take a lot of time and energy to turn that around.

They talked more about the shop and James's decision not to go back to university, and James explained to his mum why he had made the decision he had. Eventually, James's mum said:

"So, what are you boys doing today?"

"Well, if it's OK with you, we want to go shopping."

"Why wouldn't that be OK with me? What are you going to buy? Anything in particular?

James and Paul looked at each other, and grabbed each other's hand.

"Don't get mad," James said.

"Why would I get mad? What have you done?"

Alfred put his hand on Alice Marsh's.

"Unless I have misread things," he said, "your son has asked his boyfriend to marry him."

James stared at him.

"How did you know?" James asked him.

"It's written all over your faces," Alfred replied.

EPILOGUE

The registry office was only around two hundred metres from the location where James had been hit by the car, but that was far from the minds of everyone who attended the wedding, particularly James and Paul.

It had been two years since Alfred had made James the offer of taking over the shop. Things had moved slower than had originally been planned, but James had finally taken over the running of the shop a few months earlier, and Alfred had delivered the official documents for the change in ownership the day before the wedding.

There were times when James had doubted that he would be up to the challenge of everything involved in running the shop, but he forged ahead with it anyway, knowing he had people around him who would help when he needed it, not least Alfred himself, who still sat behind the desk once or twice a week, reading from his Sherlock Holmes book. Alfred was back in good health, but didn't regret passing on the shop. He felt the time was right to take some time for himself and to stop having the pressure of having to open the shop every day.

When she had first found out about the engagement, Alice Marsh was both happy and worried. The boys had been only eighteen, after all. She encouraged them to think about what they were doing, and to make sure it was definitely what they wanted, but there was never really any chance that they would change their minds. Now, two years later, it was their big day.

It was a small wedding. James had members of his family there, but Paul only had a distant uncle and aunt. His mum had been invited, but didn't reply to the invitation. Paul had secretly hoped that she would turn up anyway, but she didn't. Paul did at least have some of his friends from work there, and James's family was *his* family.

James had kept in touch with Adam from university, who had come to visit on a couple of occasions and had got on well with Paul, too, despite the fear that there would be some awkwardness between them. Adam sat in the third row with his boyfriend of four months. He still hadn't come out to his parents. He wanted to, but he just wasn't ready for it, and neither were they.

Also present were Andrew and Jonathan. Andrew had returned to work after two months, and had been as well as could be expected ever since. Medication helped, as did counselling, but Jonathan was the one who helped more than anything else. There were still rough days, sometimes rough weeks or months, but they got through them, and they too were now thinking seriously of getting engaged.

On the day before the wedding, James and Paul had received a bunch of flowers from Jason and Madeline. The fallout with Rick and Mark had only been temporary, and the poker nights had eventually continued, with Badger never appearing again. Jason had finished his courses at college and was now applying to university to study Art. He and Madeline had both applied to the same places, in the hope they could find somewhere that would accept both of them, and they could share a house or flat between them.

It was James and Paul's big day, but one look at everyone gathered in the room might have made you think that the happiest person there was the best man, and perhaps he was. For James and Paul, there was only one person who could fulfil that role, and Alfred McKechnie was moved to tears when they asked him if he would do it. Now, he stood there, the rings in his pocket ready for his big moment, and he couldn't be prouder of the two young men who walked down the aisle towards him.

THE END

Also available!

A Ghost of a Chance, a stand-alone ghostly romance which reunites audiences with Luke and Jane, first featured in *Breaking Point.*

Sample the opening of the book on the next page.

A GHOST OF A CHANCE

CHAPTER 1

The argument wasn't the beginning of it. That had been a few months earlier, although I wasn't aware of it at the time. But, without the argument, the rest of my story would not have taken place.

I was in my room, laying on the bed listening to my mum and step-dad get more and more heated as they "discussed" me in the kitchen – which they seemed to have forgotten was right underneath my bedroom. I had been discussed a lot lately and, at first, this occasion looked like it was going to be no different to any other.

"I don't care how much the holiday cost, Gerald," my mum was saying. "We can't go and leave Chet on his own for a whole week. Not at the moment. Not how he is."

"This isn't about the money. Don't you think he might be happy about having the place to himself? It will give him room to breathe."

"He doesn't need room to breathe. He needs looking after."

"He has depression, not Alzheimer's. You can't smother him, Sandra."

I adjusted my position on the bed so that my knees were tucked up under my chin. Well, not literally under my chin – at six feet four, my legs are too long for that. But you get the idea.

I kept my eyes shut, imagining exactly what was going on in the kitchen below. I knew that Mum would be leaning up against one of the worktops, probably flapping a tea towel around as she got more and more annoyed. My step-dad, meanwhile, would be sitting down at the dining table, trying to remain calm - and trying to get comfortable on those God-awful dining chairs with the slats at the back that make your back ache like hell when you've sat on them for all of two minutes. I don't know why they ever bought them. They must have tried them out in the shop. I would say they bought them online, but Mum would never even think about buying furniture on the internet. "I like to see what I'm buying," Mum always says.

Mum would have been hurt by the suggestion that she had been smothering me. However, the problem was that she *had* been smothering me ever since the trip to the doctors when I had been diagnosed with depression. More on that later. But really, it was like being in prison and on suicide watch. What she didn't understand was that I wasn't suicidal. I understood why she was worried I might be, but I wasn't.

She had no idea how thankful I had been that we were living in a bigger house. My bedroom was now big enough that I only ever had to leave it to eat and use the bathroom – and I even tried my best to keep both of those activities down to a minimum.

I never thought I'd get to live in a house like that – and I wouldn't have if Mum hadn't got married to my step-dad. *Gerald.* The name made you think of a fifty year old man with a hairy chest, shades, and a medallion. Sadly, the description fit Gerald rather well.

For the first fourteen years of my life, me, Mum and Dad had lived in a small two-bedroomed terraced house. My room had been tiny. There was barely room for a bed and a wardrobe. In fact, my feet had kept hitting the side of the wardrobe when I was in bed. It's that six-feet-four problem again.

Now we were in a four-bedroomed house. It was even detached. And there was a small swimming pool in the back garden. OK, it wouldn't take many strokes to get from one end to the other. Ok, it was essentially an overgrown bath, but that was hardly the point.

Mum could never have afforded this house – she could barely afford the last place. I don't think Gerald could have afforded it either if hadn't been so cheap. None of us had yet worked out why the price was so low. There had been no murders there. I'd checked the internet and the newspaper archives at the library.

Now Gerald wanted to take Mum on a holiday. He had booked it as a treat and they were meant to be leaving the following week, but since I'd been diagnosed with depression, Mum wasn't willing to leave me. As I said, suicide watch.

"I'm not smothering him," Mum continued. "I'm worried that he'll…"

"Do something stupid?"

"Yes!"

I heard the dining chair scrape across the floor as Gerald stood up, no doubt walking over to put his arm around her – or something equally predictable. Or perhaps his back just ached from those bloody dining chairs.

"Sandra, he wouldn't need to be alone for that to happen. He could do it any time."

Thanks, Gerald. Make her feel better, why don't you?

"He could do it with us in the next room," he went on. "Are you going to hide up all the knives, razor blades, pills and rope just to make sure he doesn't do it?"

"Do you think I should?"

"*No*, of course not. You could be walking beside him on the street and he could still throw himself in front of a bus. You can't wrap him in cotton wool. He needs to be able to work through this by himself."

Mum must have hated hearing this. She hated being told what to do at the best of times, and she wasn't going to back down if she could help it.

She had no idea how much I wanted them to just bugger off for the week and leave me in peace. Bliss. I'd never been left alone in the house for more than one night, and the thought of being alone for a whole week sounded like heaven. No suicide watch for a whole seven days.

"I can't believe you really want to abandon him for a week, Gerald. After everything he's been through."

"I'm not abandoning him. I'm saying you can't watch over him for twenty-four hours a day. Besides, he'd probably be glad to have the house to himself for a few days. Have some friends over."

"What friends? Have you ever seen any of his friends? Have you heard the phone ringing day and night with them asking how he is?"

She had a point. The phone had hardly been ringing off the wall – not that phones are even attached to walls these days.

"He probably speaks to them on Facebook or Twitter or Skype. He's sixteen. He's got friends."

"He's *gay*, Gerald."

"And you think that stops him having friends? It's 2016. No-one gives a shit about whether he's gay or not. He's gay, not Donald Trump."

The comparison seemed a little strange, but it is true to say that one was a reason for being hated more than other. At least, it was in my part of the country. I can't vouch for elsewhere.

"The decision is made," my mum said firmly. "We're not leaving him alone. It's up to me to decide. I'm his mother."

"And you forget that *I'm* his father."

And *he'd* forgotten that I was upstairs and heard what he had just said.

Gerald wasn't my step-dad. He was my *dad*.

CHAPTER 2

I got up off the bed and walked over to the shelves of CDs and records that lined the other side of the room. I picked out a John Coltrane album, rather imaginatively called *Coltrane*, and took the record out of its sleeve. Placing it on the turntable, I gently lowered the stylus on to the first track.

Jazz is in my blood. My parents had named me "Chet" after Chet Baker, the jazz trumpeter and vocalist who rose to fame during the early 1950s.

There had been moments when I had wondered whether they did this in the rather vain hope that I might look as beautiful as my namesake had when *he* was young. Chet Baker on the front of an LP cover, looking at the camera rather seductively in a James Dean-like way was, after all, my first real crush. It had seemed odd being attracted to the man I was named after and, thankfully, that phase of my life soon passed.

The next phase was worse, however, with me worrying that I might end up like the older Baker: drug-addicted and haggard, with his looks completely gone, and his face more resembling a Chinese Shar-Pei dog than James Dean.

The final phase was the one where I thought I might meet the same fate as my namesake: dead on the pavement outside a hotel room. Luckily, though, I've never been tempted by drugs. I now have to take so many for medicinal purposes that I think that it has put me off even trying them. As for alcohol, I don't much like the taste of beer, and so probably won't turn into an alcoholic either. I don't even stay in hotels very often, so throwing myself out of a hotel window seemed somewhat unlikely. That phase passed too.

My love of jazz was something my parents had passed on to me. Their enthusiasm for it had always been great. I grew up in a home where Duke Ellington, Miles Davis and Ella Fitzgerald were constantly being played. The hi-fi was on more than the TV.

That had changed when Dad left, though. Mum rarely played any music after that. Gerald doesn't even like jazz. He thinks it's a "noise."

But my upbringing had now been screwed with. The problem was that I had now suddenly learned that the man I had called "Dad" for sixteen years wasn't actually my dad after all – and Gerald, my step-dad, was my real father.

It was almost funny. On the one hand, Mum was desperate to watch over me and wrap me in cotton wool, and yet, on the other hand, she had just dropped a bombshell that could have completely screwed me up.

No wonder Mum had been so insistent on trying to get me to call her new husband "Dad" instead of Gerald. He *was* Dad!

I went back and laid down on the bed, my hands folded underneath my head, and looked up at the ceiling. With a family like mine it was little surprise I ended up being diagnosed with depression.

Actually, that's rather unfair. My depression wasn't caused by anything that Mum had done, or anything that Gerald had done, or even by Mum and Dad splitting up.

No, it was all triggered by Jeremy.

CHAPTER 3

Jeremy Wilson had joined the school about eighteen months before, when I was nearly fifteen.

There was no big announcement. Normally when there was a new addition to the class, whether at the beginning of a school year or mid-way through, the pupil in question would be encouraged to stand up and introduce themselves. That didn't happen with Jeremy. In fact, very few of the class even talked about him. He just appeared at the beginning of Year 10 and, to most, he might as well have been invisible.

For most new kids, that would probably have been a blessing, but I always felt a bit sorry for Jeremy back then. He sat a few rows from the front of the class in each lesson, slouching in his seat slightly in what appeared to be an unconscious effort not to be noticed. He seemed to have an air of sadness, of melancholy, about him.

Despite Jeremy's striking features and handsome, if slightly brooding, face, the girls at school didn't swoon over him. In most cases, at least some of them would normally have tried to have got his attention, but for some reason that didn't happen.

I, meanwhile, desperately *did* want to get the attention of Jeremy. Whenever we were in the same class, I found my eyes wandering over to where he sat, and I switched off from what the teacher was saying or what I was meant to be doing, and just watched him. I knew that Jeremy wasn't totally unaware of this – sometimes he looked back at me, giving the slightest hint of a smile or a nod that sent shivers down my spine. And yet, when our paths crossed in the corridor or outside and I said "hi," Jeremy never took the chance to engage in conversation. In fact, he almost seemed scared of me, but I couldn't work out why.

In the changing rooms, I found it even more difficult to take my eyes of him, savouring the few seconds each week that I got to see Jeremy's bare chest as he changed from his school shirt into his football shirt and back again. One week, Jeremy looked back across at me, and I could have sworn that he winked at me. But that couldn't have been possible. It must have been in my imagination.

Jeremy was a complete loner – not, I found out later, because people didn't want to be his friend, but because he didn't want to be theirs. He liked being alone. He once told me that he never understood why no-one could get it that not everyone wanted to be surrounded by people all the time. Some people just liked being alone. I knew what he meant. I felt the same way. We understood each other. From the moment I met him, the only person I wanted to spend time around was Jeremy – and that was before we'd even spoken to each other.

It was jazz that eventually brought us together. He'd been at the school about six months by then, but we'd barely spoken – just the occasional "hi" when we passed each other in the corridor. I'd wanted to get to know him, but had never worked out how to start the conversation.

I'd taken my iPod into school and had been listening to it one lunchtime. He'd walked past me and heard the music that was leaking out of the earphones. He tapped me on the shoulder.

"Is that Ellington?" he asked. "Newport, 1956?"

I told him it was. My life was never the same again.

A friendship was born. No, not just a friendship. A really close bond. Very quickly, we became almost inseparable: two loners together. We sat together in class at school whenever we could, and then he'd come to my house afterwards and we'd spend hours together listening to jazz. All kinds of jazz. We'd educate each other on our passion for the music:

"Have you heard this?"

"What do you make of this?"

"This is just my favourite piece of music ever. Have a listen."

It was bliss. We were soul mates.

After we'd known each other for a few months, we were lying together on my bed listening to *Hello Love*, an album of ballads by Ella Fitzgerald. Stan Getz was playing a solo. Jeremy turned slowly towards me and kissed me on the cheek. It was so gentle. So soft that I hardly felt it at all. Just a hesitant brush of his lips on my face.

Jeremy had taken a gamble. He didn't know how I'd react or if I felt the same way. He didn't even know if I liked guys. He needn't have worried. I *did* feel the same way. From then on, we were boyfriends, although none of our family or other friends (if Jeremy had other friends) were even aware that we were gay. We didn't discuss being boyfriends with each other either. It was just something that happened naturally and we didn't question it.

When we weren't listening to jazz, we were talking excitedly about the house we would one day live in together, and how one of the rooms would be our music room, and how our records and CDs would line the walls. There would be a couple of plush sofas, so we could just sit or lay there in comfort, wallowing in the music we so loved. On other occasions, we spoke of how we'd go to the same university when we had got through sixth form.

It was all so perfect.

Then, out of the blue, came the phone call.

A Ghost of a Chance is available in paperback and Kindle formats from all Amazon stores and other selected online retailers.

Printed in Great Britain
by Amazon